ALEX LA GUMA was born i[...] [...]ding figures in the black lib[...] [...]ment. As a young man he joined the Communist Party, and was a member of its Cape Town district committee until 1950, when it was banned. In 1956 he helped to organize the South African representatives who drew up the Freedom Charter, and consequently was among the 156 accused at the Treason Trials of the same year. In 1960 he began writing for *New Age*, a progressive newspaper, and in 1962 was put under house arrest. Before his five-year sentence could elapse, a No Trial Act was passed and he and his wife were put into solitary confinement. On their release from prison, they returned to house arrest, eventually fleeing to Britain in 1967. They moved to Cuba, where La Guma was the ANC representative. He died in 1985.

Alex La Guma's first work was *A Walk in the Night* (1962), a collection of short stories. It was followed by *And a Threefold Cord, The Stone Country, In the Fog of the Seasons' End* and *Time of the Butcherbird*.

TIME OF THE BUTCHERBIRD

ALEX LA GUMA

TIME OF
THE BUTCHERBIRD

HEINEMANN

Heinemann Educational Publishers
Halley Court, Jordan Hill, Oxford OX2 8EJ
A Division of Reed Educational & Professional Publishing Limited

Heinemann: A Division of Reed Publishing (USA) Inc.
361 Hanover Street, Portsmouth, NH 03801-3912, USA

Heinemann Publishers (Pty) Limited
PO Box 781940, Sandton 2146, Johannesburg, South Africa

OXFORD   MELBOURNE   AUCKLAND
JOHANNESBURG   BLANTYRE   GABORONE
IBADAN   PORTSMOUTH (NH) USA   CHICAGO

First published in the African Writers Series in 1979
Reprinted 1986
First published in this edition, 1987

British Library Cataloguing in Publication Data

La Guma, Alex
Time of the Butcherbird.
(African writers series).
I. Title II. Series
823[F] PR9369.3.L3

ISBN 0-435-90758-1

Printed and bound in Great Britain by
Cox & Wyman Ltd, Reading, Berkshire

00   01   02   03   12   11   10   9

When the government trucks had gone, the dust they had left behind hung over the plain and smudged the blistering afternoon sun so that it appeared as a daub of white-hot metal through the moving haze. The dust hung in the sky for some time before settling down on the white plain. The plain was flat and featureless except for two roads bull-dozed from the ground, bisecting each other to lie like scars of a branded cross on the pocked and powdered skin of the earth. In the distance a new water tank on metal stilts jutted like an iron glove clenched against the flat and empty sky. The dust settled slowly on the metal of the tank and on the surface of the brackish water it contained, laboriously pumped from below the sand; on the rough cubist mounds of folded and piled tents dumped there by officialdom; on the sullen faces of the people who had been unloaded like the odds and ends of furniture they had been allowed to bring with them, powdering them grey and settling in the perspiring lines around mouths and in the eye sockets, settling on the unkempt and travel-creased clothes, so that they had the look of scarecrows left behind, abandoned in this place. A hand experimentally dug up some sand and let it trickle away again through horny fingers, dropping between patched and squatting knees, to return to the earth. This was no land for ploughing and sowing; it was not even good enough to be buried in. The people stood in the afternoon burn of the molten-metal sun, the scorching air turning the sweat and dust to plaster on their faces. They shuffled in the dust and gradually dispersed a little way from one another, looking about speculatively. An infant wailed thirstily in the sling on a mother's back, a child complained, someone spat out dust and hummed the opening bars of a song; another joined in and after a while everybody was singing. At least one could sing in this wretched and deserted land.

*

It's time I traded this bus in for something new, Edgar Stopes thought. The old station-wagon shuddered and rattled on the road, and when he speeded up he heard the rattle turn into a metallic

1

hammering. Must be a bearing, he thought, although he had had enough oil put in at the last place he had stopped. Nothing to do but take it easy until the next stop: nurse her along. Damn it, it would add hours to his trip. He would get in when everything was shut down and it would mean having to stay the night at that filthy hotel. But there was nothing else to do but slacken down to a speed that would reduce the strain on whatever the hell it was buggering about, and hope the old bus didn't break down completely, go kaput here in the middle of bloody nowhere.

The station-wagon trembled along and he looked out across the dusty landscape for signs which might indicate that he was nearing his destination. Towards the west the sun was a brassy smear in the dusty blue sky. In the distance a passenger train horned its way northward. The tyres rumbled on the asphalt surface of the secondary road at this slow speed. They were quite new tyres, but he told himself that fitting them had not made any difference to the ageing of the engine, the loosening of springs, rods, belts. We're getting on in years, he thought, grinning slightly: we're crocked up. The low speed reduced the flow of air through the open window and he felt the sweat gather again under his clothes.

The landscape trembled by: red, red-brown, yellow-red, pink, and it was with relief that he saw the first signs of habitation for many hours trudging into view, although it was only a line of black men at the side of the road, shovels carried like rifles on tattered shoulders. They did not waver as the car passed them, but trudged on with a sort of fixed purpose. A stretch of gravel and the red dust boiled up like a flame-shot smokescreen so he had to turn the window up. Heat enclosed him in a cocoon of perspiration. One more stop and it's Home James, Edgar Stopes thought, for what it's worth. He did not think of home as somewhere there was rest, comfort, a chance to invite friends over for dinner or a drink, to sit by the radio and listen to the rugby commentary. Home was just another place where you had to stop off only to have a bath, change your suit, a quick shot before checking in at the Head Office. Home was Maisie with screen magazines and sullen mouth. Anything else was mere trimmings, like the metal hub-caps on the wheels of the station-wagon, the nigger doll hanging by its neck above the middle of the windscreen.

In front of the dust-powdered windscreen the road speared the scorched countryside. A few miles unreeled slowly and, at last, here was the railway-crossing, the boom, and he was bumping across the tracks, nursing the car all the time, a little anxious that something would not go wrong now that he was within reach of repair. But he found time to wave to the man in the signal-box — one had to maintain goodwill all the time. The man waved back, recognising the station-wagon and its driver, the pale brown hair falling back from the scalp, the pink face starting to go pudgy, the near-blond moustache that surmounted the wide, seemingly humorous mouth.

Rounding the curve in the road and out of the sight of the signal-box again, Edgar Stopes passed a black man sitting on the verge at the roadside, wriggling bare toes while he examined one of the boots he had taken off. Past the man the edge of the country came into sight in the fading afternoon: a huddle of whitewashed railway cottages with chickens scrabbling in the dooryards, an empty sheep-pen, a blistered shearing-shed. Shadows were starting to surround things now. Still dropping west the sun flared like an explosion, late afternoon heat dancing above the steeple, quivering along the flat top of the yellow-brown hillside with the name of the place spelled out in whitewashed boulders.

Beyond the railway houses the town's only service station displayed its petrol pumps and dusty flags, and Edgar Stopes ran the station-wagon onto the concrete apron in front of the workshop where a battered farm pick-up truck had been disembowelled, surrounded by spare parts, pools of grease and strewn tools. He sounded the horn and climbed out, wiping perspiration from his face.

Ahead of him the town street lay quiet under the last of another sweltering day, hanging out its shadows with relief in front of the Railway Hotel; a line of whitewashed houses behind burnt hedges: around a speckled car and a wagon in front of the feed store, heads of mules drooping; from the Boer War monument in the dusty square and the face of the old church with its red concrete steps. The sun was beginning to take shape now above the flat crest of the hill with its whitewashed boulders, slowly contracting into a disc of quivering red, like heated roundshot. An old coloured man came out of the feed store and commenced to sweep the sidewalk with a reed broom, and from the direction of the square a boy on a bicycle raised the wake of red dust, unnecessarily ringing his way along the otherwise deserted street.

Edgar Stopes leaned over and sounded the horn again and a man came from the dimness of the workshop, wiping his hands on a tangle of cotton waste. He had the paunchy heaviness and the thick muscles of a blacksmith under the sweat-stained singlet and dirty overalls, red down on his powerful forearms matched the cropped hair on his head and he smiled with big, yellowish teeth out of a wrinkled, skinning, sunburnt face.

Edgar Stopes said, 'Afternoon, *middag* Klaas. How goes it?' He spoke the Afrikaans language with a slight hesitation which came basically from reluctance. Here in the countryside he was like a foreigner and he had learnt that he would make no headway with these people unless he submitted to their narrow arrogance. He considered himself a broadminded man: Live and let live, but why in hell couldn't a man talk his own language instead of having to struggle with their mumbo-jumbo? After all he belonged as much as they did, and above all he was doing them a service. Yet in order to maintain goodwill, to obtain the orders of plastic combs, drag chains, electric light bulbs, he had to surrender his identity, become a bad imitation of one of these bloody Dutchmen. He wiped his moustache with his grubby handkerchief and grinned at the red-haired man who was saying, 'Back again in our part of the world, *neh*? How's the old bus?'

'Just managed to get her here', Edgar Stopes said. 'The blerry thing started — how do you call it now — rattling like a bogger. Bearing trouble I reckon.'

The red-haired man circled the station-wagon and unlatched the bonnet, peered at the engine. He said without looking up, 'Start her up a little, Mister Stopes, and we'll listen to her.'

Edgar Stopes climbed back into the car and started the motor, speeded it up. 'Can you hear it?'

The red-haired man listened. He did something to the engine and instructed, 'Put up the spark and then idle her a little. Now accelerate.' He listened for a while and then straightened up, closing the bonnet. '*Ja*. I reckon it must be bearing trouble, hey. Maybe the oil does not get to the bearings.' He wiped his hands on the cotton waste again while Edgar Stopes climbed out and asked, 'She's kaput? Can you fix her?'

'You have to leave her,' the red-haired man told him. 'Got to be drained so I can look at the matter properly. Maybe anything, I reckon.'

'Done more than fifteen thousand miles. I reckon that counts too, hey.'

The red-haired man grinned. 'Try trading her in, but I think not

4

that you'll get much these times.

Edgar Stopes said, 'Well, man, can you work on her so I can have her by tomorrow? Got some orders to take in town, and then I'll be on my way to the Head Office.'

'Tomorrow?' The red-haired man shook his head. 'Not tomorrow, *meneer*. Day after, ja. But tomorrow all business will be closed here most of the day. No shops open, nothing. You will have to stay until the following day, if I can't fix it in the afternoon.'

'Closed?' Edgar Stopes asked in surprise. 'Why then? I don't remember that it's a holiday.'

'No, not a holiday exactly,' the red-haired man laughed. 'No, tomorrow there will be a special church service — to pray for rain. You have seen the drought, *mos*. The whole country is going to pray for rain, and everything will be closed down until after the service, mostly until the afternoon. Everybody will go to the service.' He shook his head. 'No, you'll do no business here tomorrow, Mister Stopes. Shops will have to close too, you see. So you will have to wait until day after tomorrow for the car, I think.'

Edgar Stopes thought, Jesus, what a waste of time. A whole day wasted, praying for bloody rain, and here I will be having to twiddle my bloody thumbs before I can take their stupid orders. The stupid bastards might not even *want* anything. Two nights in this bloody one-horse town. He wiped his sweating neck and put on a smile for the red-haired man. 'Well, reckon there's nothing I can do about it, neh? One day is not too bad. I can have a rest, not true?'

'Ja, perhaps you can do that. It's a good idea.

'Well, let me get my bags.'

He went around to the back of the station-wagon, thinking angrily, Praying for rain, by Jesus. He opened the rear of the vehicle and dragged out the sample bag and his suitcase. The red-haired man said, 'First thing I will see to her; it will be awright.' He took the keys from the salesman. 'I think not that there's anybody else staying at the hotel. I tell you what, maybe later tonight I will come over and tell you something definite.'

'Good idea, good idea,' Edgar Stopes said, moving away with a bag in each hand, his suit sweat-stained and wrinkled, his mouth bitter below the almost-blond moustache. He twitched his head cheerily in greeting, putting on the smile, and walked away from the service station, heading for the hotel with its imitation Dutch-colonial front, his mind saying, The bloody *things* I have to put up with in this business. Praying for bloody rain, of all things. He hardly ever read a newspaper so he knew nothing about it, and he grinned sourly, If I could take orders for rain I might make a packet all right, but you don't travel in rain, you travel in hairpins, greeting cards, French letters, cough-drops. UNIVERSAL PRODUCTS — Anything From A Needle To An Anchor. But no rain, he thought cynically, who needs rain? Not me, I don't need rain. What I need right now is a bath and a long beer. His underclothes felt sticky and his blue tropical suit clung damply to his armpits and thighs, and out in the open the motionless air surrounded him like a blanket in spite of the advancing shadows.

A man in untidy khaki and felt hat came out of the feed store, climbed into his dusty car and drove away towards the square. The mules twitched in their harness and drooped their heads while Edgar Stopes passed, lugging his bags towards the Railway Hotel. Up the street in front of the magistrate's office which was near the police station, two black men in shabby clothes made twin shadows on the dust of the square.

The front of the Railway Hotel was draped with shadow. The plastic tables and chairs in the area behind a tawdry hedge at the side of the taproom were deserted, and the entrance between shaded windows and clumsily whitewashed walls led to welcome shadows that fell along more whitewash, an old hallstand, a railway timetable, a faded picture of the Drakensberg, another of the State President; a small counter with a brass spittoon on the floor before it. Windowed doors that led on the left to the tiny dining-room, on the right to the taproom. Straight ahead, beside the counter, another doorway curtained with fly-specked strings of wooden beads gave way to a short narrow passage with the kitchen off it and stairs to the four cramped bedrooms above. To all this Edgar Stopes was familiar. He knew that the whitewash would come off on your clothes if you were not careful, that the coloured help was named Fanie, that mice occupied the thatch roof. He had passed this way many times in the cause of Universal Products, and now, taking off his sunglasses in the dim hallway, he did not savour having to spend a whole day in this place, with the meaningless chatter about Merino sheep, the town's prospects in the provincial country-sports meeting, the never-forgotten plan for the asphalting of the square.

Rapping the counter with sweaty knuckles, he knew that the manager's wife would appear with her shrill and nerve-pinching laughter, her tight-clamped grey bun, and sure enough, there she was coming out of the dining-room. A small birdlike woman with grey-brown hair drawn tight around the sharp red face, the frail body hidden in dark cloth like widow's weeds, although her husband still flourished behind the bar in the taproom, her thin, red, clawlike hands fluttering, while she screamed like a jaybird. ' *'O, dis Meneer Stopes.* Again back with us, hey? How goes it then? We was expecting you. I said to Hendrik, I said, that Meneer Stopes will be arriving any day now. But is it not hot? *Aitog,* this heat.' She shrilled with laughter at him.

She flitted to the back of the counter while Edgar Stopes said, putting on his business smile, 'Ja, here I am again, Missus Kroner, here I am again. How goes it with you?'

'O, not too bad, it's only my joints.' The scream of laughter while she produced the register. 'Not so young as I was. We're heading towards the old side, neh?'

Edgar Stopes asked, taking up the ballpoint she offered, 'Is it true everything is closed tomorrow? I'll have to stay over a day?'

'Everything will be closed until after the service, Mister Stopes. It's the drought, you understand, all this heat.' But heat, the drought, painful joints, did not seem to affect her; she was as shrill as ever: 'We must but ask our living Lord to bring the rain. The sheep are dying, the river dried up, the dam empty. Number three, you can have number three. Sommerman lost half his flock these last few months.' She screeched with laughter, as if she found some grotesque humour in disaster. 'Everybody's going to the service and I reckon the Dominee Visser will have a beautiful sermon to preach. No, there won't be business tomorrow until the service is over. Well, you can stay the day with us, neh?'

'It will be a chance to rest,' Edgar Stopes said with his false sweaty smile. 'Anybody else staying here?'

'Well, Hannes Meulen has taken a room. You know Mister Meulen? *Oupa* Johannes' grandson? But he went to the city for a little time, just come in on the train. You know he's going to stand for the *Volksraad*.' Edgar Stopes did not know who the hell she was talking about but he smiled, nodding, 'Yes, yes, I remember him now.' It was all public relations. The woman's screaming got on his nerves and he wanted to get upstairs and take a bath. 'There's water for a bath?' he asked. He wasn't going to pay these bloody Dutchmen a whole day's rent if there was no bath.

'O, ja, you can bath. It's only the garden which cannot be

watered. No water for the garden for months now. We must save water, the Provincial Council told us. All the flowers have died.' She screamed with laughter again, her little grey eyes bright as precious drops in the thin face.

'Let's hope that it rains,' Edgar Stopes said, as the woman turned the birdlike head with its tight bun like a crest towards the beaded curtain and screamed:

'Fanie, *vorento,* come forward.' Then to Edgar Stopes 'The Lord Jesus will provide, we must but trust in the living Lord for everything.' She screamed again, 'Fanie. Where's that *bliksem?* You sitting in the shade again when there's work to do?'

Somebody called, 'I'm here, *nooi,* here I am, Mies Kroner.' The beads clashed and a middle-aged coloured man wearing a soiled canvas apron over an old shirt and trousers emerged, bobbing his head at the landlady and the guest.

The woman said, 'Lord, must I always be shouting my lungs out after you? Take the boss's bags up to number three and see you open the window to let some air in.' She smiled again at Edgar Stopes with small white teeth, 'Sorry I cannot see you to your room myself, Meneer Stopes, but it's my joints. My joints trouble me a lot these days. There will be *soesaties* for supper, we do however get a piece of mutton now and then in spite of the drought, soesaties and rice.' She screamed again with laughter and Edgar Stopes, following the houseboy through the bead curtains thought: Joints — it's your bloody voice should trouble you more often.

At the end of the short passage the open back door let in a rectangle of harsh sunlight and the view of a section of withered, sunbaked garden. It was cooler inside the hotel, in spite of the cramped space, and climbing the narrow stairs behind the man with the bags Edgar Stopes itched for the touch of cold water.

The dim room upstairs which the houseboy unlocked was like the one he had slept in on another occasion... the same whitewashed walls, the railway picture of spiny aloes framed over the dressing-table, and there was a crack in the wardrobe mirror. The iron single bed might have been bought second-hand from a hospital.

The houseboy put down the bags and went over to raise the spring-blind and open the window to let in a rush of hot yellow air, while Edgar Stopes sitting wearily on the bed cover said, 'Pull down the blind, man, you want to roast me in here?' He mopped his neck and asked, 'Can you bring me a bottle of beer? Cold beer, hey.' The houseboy shifted on his sandalled feet and said, 'The bar only open half-past five, master.'

'Jussus,' Edgar Stopes groaned. 'Half-past five.' He looked at his wrist-watch. 'Awright, bring me a beer as soon as it opens. I will take a bath in the meantime. Cold beer, remember.' He felt in his coat pocket and drew out a change purse, rummaged in it and then gave the houseboy a small coin. 'Here's a tip for you. Don't forget the beer.'

The man bobbed and smiled, 'I won't, master, I won't forget.'

Alone in the shaded room, Edgar Stopes opened a suitcase on the bed. If that ... bus hadn't performed, I could've been here earlier and off home by evening. To be stuck here in the *bundu* again with all these bloody Dutchmen. They're not like us, modern, up-to-date. Be damned if I'll go to their bloody service. What you need is a quick way to make a few thousand and start all over again, and goodbye Dolly Gray to all this.

He unpacked irritably, finding among the soiled and crumpled linen his last set of underwear and a clean shirt he had managed to save. He thought, Well at least there's no blooming Maisie with her snide remarks. What could be more petulant than a second-rate chorus girl who believed she was a star and should be out front under the lights? To his surprise there was a half jack of brandy he had forgotten about. Well this will certainly make my night.

Stripped down, he wrapped himself in a thin dressing-gown and went out to the hallway, carrying his shaving kit. Down below he heard Mrs Kroner's shrill voice again. When he shut himself into the cramped bathroom with its stained walls he found that the water pumped from the railway station was far from cold, but tepid and brown, flecked with rust, and he sat on the edge of the tub with his limp hair, near-blond moustache and bitter mouth, thinking, What a world, what a bloody world, as if his small thoughts encompassed all the problems of life.

*

The office of the Bantu Commissioner was one of a row enclosing the few administrative units of the town: the management board, the electricity supply commission, the water board. They all had glass double-doors shaded with plain curtains bleached to an unidentifiable colour by the sun. Only the police station at the end of the little arcade presented a brick front and solid teak doors, although the varnish had blistered. All were joined by a verandah, forming the base for the magistrate's court which was upstairs. The whole faced the dusty square which was flanked for the rest by the church and a few small shops.

The two black men stood in the bright, hot sunlight that moved across the gravel of the square outside the Bantu Commissioner's office, and one of them straightened his yellowed, cracked panama hat, saying, 'I said all the time that they would not listen to our words.'

'But you told him, the Commissioner, you told him.' the other said. 'The great white lord, the elephant.' He laughed shortly and derisively. A few birds fluttered from the direction of the parched oaks across the square and settled on the edge of the verandah. 'They are as concerned as *those*,' he said.

The two men were both middle-aged and poorly dressed and carried walking-sticks cut from branches, and they had put on old, frayed neckties for the occasion, as well as fastened all the remaining buttons of their jackets. The poverty of their dress — the frayed cuffs and the wrinkled shirts (the one in the panama hat had also added a collar pin)—had been given a sort of despairing dignity by these gestures. One had to show that one was as dignified as *they* were.

Before they had gone into the Commissioner's office earlier, they had mopped the perspiration from their faces for they had walked a long time. They had found the waiting-room as usual: the front bare and empty except for a wooden bench against the wall beside the shaded glass door, and behind the rail the clerk who sat at a desk and tapped at a typewriter, read what he had typed, frowned and gnawed a knuckle. He wore a sports shirt open at the neck, revealing whisps of blonde hair, and he did not look up at the two men who had come in. An electric fan on a corner shelf hummed and turned its head from side to side at regular intervals. The two men had not sat down on the bench to wait as was expected, but had gone up to the partition, holding their sticks. They had taken off their old hats, and they waited stolidly for the clerk to give them some attention.

A minute twitched by on the silent electric clock on the wall, and then the man with the panama hat, who was the older of the two, had deliberately dropped his stick with a clatter.

The clerk looked up with a scowl. He could smell them, the smell of sweat and dust, and he put it down to the usual *kaffir* smell. It did not occur to him that they had walked a long way in the heat; to the

10

clerk all kaffirs smelled. He had intended to make them wait until he felt himself ready — that was the way one had to deal with these people. He said: 'Why are you not waiting until you are called? What is it? Passes? Your tax should have been paid last month already.'

The older man spoke over the rail while he groped for his stick: 'Not passes, or the tax. We have come about the moving.'

'Moving? You are Hlangeni's people? But the big boss has already spoken to you people.'

'There is a letter,' the older man said. 'It came from those in the city and said that everything about the matter would be conveyed care of this office.'

'Letter?' the clerk had asked, frowning. 'Can you read?'

'I can read,' the man had replied, smiling gravely.

Outside, the sun shifted in the square. The clerk had stood up, saying, 'Wait here.' He had edged through a door in the back of the office and the two men had waited. A fly trapped between the shade and the glass of the front door made a sawing sound, and time jerked along on the clock. Then the clerk had held the door open again to let the Commissioner through.

The Commissioner, who was also the local magistrate, peered at the two men. He did not go near because fastidiously he too wished to avoid the odour of travel that clung to them. Except for the alpaca jacket which he wore in the office, he was a model of starched and expensive neatness from his lean skull to the gleaming toes of his formal shoes. The heat, now or at any time, did not seem to affect him, and he looked tireless and enduring as a camel in a desert. His shirt collar glowed with a sheen not unlike that which covered his jowls, waxy red and blue with a network of burst blood-vessels, and he had looked at the two shabby men as if expecting that they should have tried better than to appear before him in such clothes as they wore.

So when he had spoken it was as if to recalcitrant children: 'Well, what are you people seeking now?'

'The letter,' the older black man had said patiently.

'Letter? What letter?'

'Your worship, a letter came saying that answers to our questions would be sent to you.' Adding wryly, 'It is so with those who govern us. We address them, they reply to the Commissioner, and the Commissioner conveys what they have said to us. It is a strange way of doing things, but who are we to talk against such ways?'

The Commissioner said from the doorway, his manner changing slightly, 'You have no right to talk like that. What is your name?'

'Kobe, my name is Kobe.'

The Commissioner held a cardboard folder in one hand and he glanced at the man and then jotted something on a sheet in the folder. 'It is Hlangeni who should have come. He is your headman.' He did not talk sharply but had added a little magisterial severity to the edge of his tone. They were all children, but one had to remind these people who one was: authority, the law, that one ruled here. Then he had looked across with surprise and suspicion when the black man had spoken again.

'Hlangeni as always, yes. But this time I was chosen.'

'Chosen? How could you be chosen?'

'All spoke and chose me to come this time.'

The lean and neatly brushed head had twitched impatiently. 'You people can never learn. I should not talk to you because you are not the headman. You are lucky that I agree to speak to you.' The folder had waggled at them. 'Now listen for the last time. It says here that you people asked the government office to set aside your removal because you claim the land you live on has always been yours. You have written three letters and even asked a lawyer in the city to talk for you. Where do you get money to waste on lawyers? But now the government has spoken again — the government speaks through me. It is written here that I should tell you finally that the removal of your people will go on as decided long ago. That is all.' He had replaced the paternally severe edge to his tone with the inexorable blade of judgement. 'That is what you can tell your people and the headman, Hlangeni. Also tell him I am angry with him because he did not come himself to hear my words.'

Kobe had said quietly, turning the old panama hat in his thick and dusty fingers, 'We shall tell Hlangeni. But there is something we must say too. It was given to us to say by those who chose us to come, your worship. It is this.' He had paused, his eyes grave, before going on. 'We have been told that we must go from our land, from the land of our ancestors. But it is a very difficult thing to uproot an old oak of many years. The roots of such a tree are very deep. Certainly one can take an axe and cut down such a tree, that is easy, but the roots remain and are very hard to dig up. So you see, the tree really remains. The tree goes on.'

'What are you talking about?' the Commissioner had asked, his eyes turning suspicious.

'That is all we have been told to say.'

'Well, I don't want to hear a lot of nonsense,' the Commissioner had said sharply.

'We will go now,' Kobe had said. 'Go well, your worship.' He had put on his yellowing hat and the one with him had stood aside, letting him go first, then they had gone out of the room into the late afternoon sunlight.

Now they stood in the square and the second man said, 'You told him.'

Kobe sighed and said, 'Yes, I told him.' He put a finger to one nostril and blew his nose in the dust. A boy on a cycle swept recklessly past them, playfully ringing his bell and spraying them with red dust, laughing jeeringly over his shoulder. They slapped dust from their old clothes and the second man murmured, 'There is little respect for age from them.'

'It is only a child,' Kobe said. 'Let us get along, it is a long way we have to walk and we should be in the village by sunset.'

'*Hauw*, but you told him,' the other man said again.

They set out across the square raising little spurts of dust that settled back in the footprints made by their old and cracked shoes.

★

The man who was sitting with his feet in the ditch at the side of the road pulled on the boots which he had taken off, and laced them up again carefully. He stood up in the dry ditch and wriggled his toes in the boots for a few more moments, and then picking up his jacket, climbed the verge of the road to the wire fence above. Over the fence the parched fields quivered in the afternoon haze. He stooped and climbed through the fence, taking care not to catch his clothes in the rusty barbed wire. He was wearing a khaki army shirt, washed many times and worn out at the collar, and almost colourless denim trousers, badly frayed at the cuffs and spotted with old stains. Only the hard boots looked in good order, and when he set out across the *veld* they crushed the brittle surface of the arid soil and kicked up little puffs of reddish dust. Ahead of the man and all around spread the long, dry, broken dusty stretches of reddish-yellow land, land broken in the distance by low rocky *koppies* and withered thorn trees. He slung his jacket over a shoulder and plodded off, trailing the cloud of dust, apparently oblivious of the sun overhead that turned the light of the world about him a cruel brass-yellow. The jacket was a cast-off top of khaki serge battledress, one of its epaulettes dangled free and an elbow had been torn. It was too hot to wear during the day.

Making his way through the dust, the man once again identified scanty landmarks which he had known a long time ago. It has not changed much, this place, he thought. It was a country of flat, weary distances scattered with stunted *karoo* bush that crumbled underfoot like rotten wood and left small hollows of red earth; a country of basalt and sandstone, and long ago, the man thought, of kudu and leopard. The green or brown mamba still slithers here among the prickly-pear cactus and the strewn ironstone, with the red spiders that blend into the parched dust from which the scrub and whitethorn sprout as if in defiance of the remorseless sun. The bushbuck or the steenbuck may still be hunted, but this is also the country of the cattle called Afrikander by the white men, although the fat-tailed sheep had grazed on the harsh grass and scrub during the good season, and long before the white people came bringing their Spanish Escorial and Saxon merinos to breed with them. In the good season the rain came quickly, like a gesture from the spirits, bearing down on the camelthorn trees, the milkbushes with their long leaves like thin spearblades, the Stone Age bread trees. Then the rain was gone and it would be the time of the honeybird and the dringo and the wagtail; of thorny aloes, cycads and the common sunflower.

The man remembered that when it had been a good year in the farmlands and the corn grown high as a man's head, and where the grass and scrubland met, the wool was thick on the backs of sheep, the white farmers and sometimes those from the towns who owned the land from afar, would gather for miles around to talk of crops and ewes, the price of clips of wool like Barkly Blue or karakul, over the sizzling *braaivleis* that the black servants passed around.

But I am not long for this place, he thought, not long. He watched the landscape as it shook and trembled in the heat haze and changed direction whenever necessary. He was sweating now. His khaki shirt darkened down his back and in the armpits. He raised the old army blouse and covered his head with it, letting it hang down over his neck. Up ahead he saw the line of stunted thorn trees which he recognised. They would be growing along the bank of the old stream bed, he knew for sure, and headed that way. The sun beat down on his back and made his head hum a little. It is strange the way you never forget a place, he told himself. Never forget. Like other things one should not forget; which one should treasure. The red dust rose from underfoot and got into his nostrils and between his lips, but he was used to fine dust, dust was nothing — there were other more important things about which a man should think.

His boots crunched the dry soil and he thought, It's funny how a man can become attached to boots. It was not usual. For all of his childhood he had gone barefoot, and most of his youth too. His feet had grown hard and horny, yet when they had given him boots to wear, he had taken to them with a sort of ironic pleasure. Of course they had felt awkward at first, and they had hurt his feet, but now he was used to them.

The sun had dropped lower towards the west and was gradually turning from a formless smudge into a disc of orange heat, and little shadows were appearing around the stunted bushes and dusty stones.

At last the man reached the line of thorn trees. Hauw, he thought, a slight smile forming on his peeling lips, they do not seem to have changed in the least. They last forever, these trees, left alone, they last forever. There was shade under the crooked trees, shadows forming a purple pattern of ragged bars and lines, and they grew at the edge of a long depression that was really the dried-up stream bed. The man sighed and slid off the edge of the waterless stream sending up a cloud of dust that hung on the air like a red fog, and sat down abruptly in the shade of the trees, his back against the crumbling ledge of bank. He dragged the khaki blouse from his head and mopped his streaming face with it, then he made a bundle of it and settled it like a cushion behind his neck. He stretched out his legs and breathed hard, before he relaxed comfortably in the sandiness of the bank.

In the shade, under tufts of spiky grass insects moved, ants and red spiders who lay in wait for them, grasshoppers that jerked into the yellow air and flicked their wings, black beetles with their brittle, shiny round backs lumbering up the slopes of fine dust around the oven-hot stones. An ant crawled out of the sunlight into the shade of a thorn branch, its jointed body lurching delicately across the powdered soil, leaving no mark or trail behind it, heading for a minute hole in a tiny ridge of earth. The man, watching its progress, thought he is going somewhere, that thing. He has somewhere to go and he knows that he is going there. He is like me, that little ant, knowing where he will go, what he will do. You should have taken your pass to the local Bantu Commissioner, the

15

man thought. That is what *they* thought you would do. They gave you a third-class rail warrant to come to this place, and said you must report to the Bantu Commissioner. But I am finished with Bantu Commissioners now, and with White people. I will do this one thing, and then I shall be finished with all people, the man thought. He watched the ant climb a tiny mountain of dust and then reach the hole. The hole was the width of a match-head, and the ant crawled into it but did not come out again.

The man climbed to his feet and stood for a while, slapping the dust from his clothes. Then he set off again, now following the course of the dry stream bed, carrying the battle-blouse across one shoulder. He was a Black man, not yet thirty, with wide, high cheekbones and a growth of short black hair along his heavy jaw-bones. Inside the sweat-stained shirt his shoulders were thick and heavy, the arms swinging from the rolled-up sleeves were heavy with muscle and his hands were hard, fingers thick and knobbly, the space between the thumb and forefinger and the hams of his hands hard and yellow with callouses, and he walked with a slight stoop as if his powerful shoulders and arms were too heavy for him. He walked on through the sand of the bottom of the dried-up stream and his feet left a wake of dust behind him.

The stream bed rambled, scattered with loose stones and withered water plants, across the parched landscape, narrow in places like a *donga* or widening into sandy striations that still held intact the undulations left by the flow of water. The man's boots broke up the little waves of soil and left a trail of shapeless footprints behind. Beyond the stream bed the shallow hollows in the land were beginning to take on a purple tinge as the sun moved further towards the horizon of faraway mountains.

Ahead of him the man heard the bleating of sheep and then a shrill, piercing whistle followed by a shout. He did not hurry towards the sounds, but walked on taking his own time to turn the bend in the stream to where it widened again into a rough, shallow circle with the usual thorn trees growing in a scanty clump on one bank, and the bottom of the dead stream scattered with weeds, prickly-pear and coarse brown grass. In the circle a few lean-looking sheep grazed from tuft to tuft, tearing at the coarse, brittle vegetation, their rough backs powdered with red sand. Licking at the roots of the sparse vegetation with dry tongues searching for moisture the tiny herd rotated, bleating feebly, while from the shade of an outcrop in the bank a hound with scarred ears and coarse mongrel coat caught with thorns stood panting, dusty head turned in the direction from which the man was coming.

The man came up to where the sheep grazed and they moved away from him bleating in protest, while the hound growled in its throat, the rough pelt twitching. From across the stream bed a voice called to the hound to back off, and looking across to the other bank the man saw that an old, tattered blanket had been stretched over the drooping branches of a thorn tree to form a canopy of shade, and in the shade the shepherd squatted on his haunches, watching him over thin arms held across his knees.

Trudging through the dust, the man saw that the shepherd wore only a pair of tattered trousers and the ruins of a felt hat. He had a skeleton-thin body that looked tough, nevertheless, dried and stringy and lasting as jerked meat, and his small, wizened face criss-crossed with wrinkles that had caught up the dust of the land so that he looked as if he had been drawn all over with red lines. White kinky hair grew down past his shrivelled ears, and he had a scanty white beard powdered red. The skinny arms resting on bony knees that jutted through the worn trousers, he sucked at an empty, long-stemmed, tall-bowled pipe, small eyes that were bright and moist as fresh raisins watching the man come up the bank.

He watched the man. The small brown eyes in the dusty eye-sockets did not move, and he sucked nonchalantly at the pipe until the man stood by him, big and heavy and making a wide shadow.

The man wiped his face with the army blouse and said, 'How are you, *madala*, old one? I remember you, you are Madonele.'

'And I remember you,' the shepherd said. 'You are the boy called Murile, whom the white farmers named Shilling. Shilling Murile.'

'White people,' the man who was called Shilling Murile said, and spat drily towards the stream bed.

The shepherd stared ahead and said, 'It was a bad thing the white man did to you and to your brother. Have you come from that place?' Then looking up, 'Sit, it is too hot to stand up, and you have walked a long way.'

'I walked from the railway station,' the man who was called Shilling Murile said, squatting down on his haunches in the shade by the old shepherd. 'I knew the way to come, from long ago.'

Madonele the shepherd sucked at his pipe and asked, 'Do you come from that place now?'

The other searched in the pockets of the battle blouse and looked away towards where the scanty herd of sheep still nuzzled among the dry hummocks in the stream bed. The hound crouched in the shade and watched them sleepily. 'Yes, from that place,' Murile said and unwrapped the rolled paper package which he pulled from a pocket. It was an orange-coloured bag and was half-filled with tobacco. 'There,' he said, holding it out to the shepherd, 'What pleasure is there sucking an empty pipe?'

'Hauw,' said the shepherd, extending cupped hands to receive the package, 'It is tobacco. It is some time since I have smoked tobacco.' He giggled almost childishly, and widening the mouth of the bag, scratched in it with thin, dusty fingers. He scooped tobacco into the tall bowl of the pipe and tamped it down carefully, taking his time, relishing the anticipation of smoking. 'I used to like the Magaliesberg tobacco,' he said reminiscently.

'This goes by the name of Boxer,' the man beside him said. He passed over a box of matches and the shepherd struck one, holding the flame to the tobacco until the match was almost consumed, almost reaching his fingertips while he puffed, blowing clouds of smoke. Then flicking the match away, he took the pipe from his mouth and said with pleasure, 'Hauw, hauw, hauw, this really is tobacco.' He turned his head aside and spat a long stream of saliva and the other man saw the stringiness of his neck muscles and the dry, scaly texture of the skin. The shepherd settled himself more comfortably on his hams, digging into the dry soil of the bank with thin scaly feet, the toes short and splayed, with toe-nails like tiny shells. He smoked on, saying nothing, gazing into the hazy distance as if he was deep in thought while he savoured the taste of tobacco. They sat like that side by side in silence, and the one who was called Shilling Murile let him smoke on, drawing from the old denims a portion of folded brown paper. He tore off a ragged rectangle from this and put the rest away, then proceeded to build himself a crude cigarette, licking the tube of brown paper its whole length to make it burn evenly.

Beyond the dry stream the sweltering land was now beginning to be painted with barred patterns of purple and lavender where the shadows crept into the hollows, and the horizon was gently dissolving into pink haze.

Eventually the shepherd Madonele spoke again, puffing contemplatively, 'It was a bad thing that the white man did to you and to your brother. Badder still was what he did to your brother.'

The other did not look at him but his eyes narrowed in his face and he picked up a stone and flung it towards the sheep. 'White men,' he said softly. 'I am finished with white people.' The sheep on the shadowy stream bed milled along slowly, bleating, raising dust,

'They are strong,' the shepherd said.

'There were people in that place who had also been put there by the white men and who said that we should fight on. I used to listen to them talking.'

The shepherd asked, 'Will you fight the white men? There is another who has come among us to talk of fighting.'

The man who was called Shilling Murile said, dragging at his cigarette, 'I will do what I have to do. That is why I came here again, old father. To do what I have to do.'

'To do what? Not to return home?'

'To do one thing,' the other said. His eyes shifted like backs of beetles in his face. 'There is no home now.'

The shepherd said, 'Since your brother is gone, does that mean there is no home, no family, people? We are all your brothers. I recall you and your brother. You were boys who had zest and always did things together. You cared for the animals together and what men are meant to do in the village. I remember when you went through the rites of manhood. You stayed away a long time and others had to be sent to find you.'

'We had found a leopard's tracks and followed it,' the other said. 'Now I do not wish to talk of those times.'

'Why not? Should we forget our ancestors too?'

'I have forgotten nothing,' the other said. 'But I do not want to talk about it.'

The sun was dropping nearer to the thin line of brown hills to the west and there was a tawny colour to the land, striped with blue and mauve; the pale ironstone scattered about and the spiny bushes that dotted the landscape all lay in their own individual shadows. The shepherd now rose and the other saw how thin he was and how the ribs showed under the scaly skin and dust. 'Let us go on,' the shepherd said. 'Old Hlangeni holds a council at sunset. But it will not be as in other times before he was reduced from chiefship to headman.'

'Hlangeni is no longer chief?'

The shepherd clucked, shaking his head, 'No longer chief. That is according to the whites. To them he is only a headman of the village now, but we all still consider him the chief.' He shook his head again. 'There are things to talk on and one should be in time. Also it is near the time to eat, although I don't know what will be in the pot.'

'I have no family,' the other man said, getting up, 'But I will go along with you since I am walking that way too.'

'Hauw,' said the shepherd. 'You remember certain things yet you have forgotten that fatherless children belong to everybody.'

'What I have to do I shall do on my own,' Murile said while the shepherd took down the blanket from the branches, and thrust his head through a hole in it, wearing it like a poncho. With a finger he wiped sweat from the band of the old hat before putting it on again. 'Come nevertheless,' he said. 'We are your people. Do what you wish afterwards.' He giggled and added slyly, 'Besides you have tobacco, young man.'

He slid down the bank on bare feet, waving a switch of stripped branchwood which he had picked up, whistling to the hound, and urging the sheep ahead. The sheep did not hurry, but ambled wearily along the stream bed, taking their cloud of dust with them, the hound loping by the old shepherd, tongue lolling. The other man picked up his blouse and followed, kicking truculently at the sand. After going some distance up the stream bed the shepherd, Madonele, said, still puffing at his pipe, 'I have heard that many bad things are done to people in that place where you have been.'

'Bad things,' the other said and his eyes were bleak. 'But one learns to wait, to remember.' The old rage nagged at his guts. 'It is better to remember and to wait, rather than to talk. In that place one got into big trouble through talking too much, so one just waited.'

'I will not talk about it then, since you wish it,' the shepherd said. But he added, almost shyly, unable to resist: 'Did you get the tobacco in that place?'

'I bought it on leaving,' said Murile. 'But it is the same stuff as the ration one gets after being there a certain time. Like the boots.'

'Hauw,' the shepherd said. 'Such boots are unheard of here. The white farmers wear boots. Here there has been little to eat, let alone the wearing of boots. Since there has been no rain many things have been bad. See, those are all the sheep our people have now, and since most of the young men had to go away to work only I am left to tend them.'

Beyond the low banks of the stream bed the distance towards the horizon was undulations of beige and tan and red-brown, separated by pale shadows. Now that the sun was on the decline some of its violence was gone, its hammering heat dissipated, although the air was hot.

'Why not dig a water hole?' Murile asked. 'There is water under this dried-up bed. If you go down far enough the water will escape upwards.'

The shepherd blew smoke and looked to where the hound was ushering the scrawny sheep. 'There was once talk of a windmill and a pump, but then the Commissioner sent the order that we are to be moved from this place. Who would give credit to such a village? Also the people have not planted much because of the order. A paper was brought with the names, and a man to mark the houses. That is what old Hlangeni is going to talk about.'

'The people have lived here since the time of our grandfathers,' the man called Shilling Murile said. 'Even before that time.' He was silent for a moment, thinking back and feeling the old rage worrying within him. 'Is not my brother buried here?'

The shepherd nodded and clicked, flicking the sand with his switch as they walked on. '*Eweh*, that is so. Your brother is buried here.'

They plodded dustily on in silence and then the hound, knowing the way, trotted up a worn cut in the bank, the sheep bleating after it. The men followed, climbing the gap and coming out into a section of low dunes and stony hillocks where thorn trees and thirsty willows, sagging exhaustedly, clung to the withering ground. There was firesmoke in the air and some of the land on the stream bank had once been cultivated, but now the dry sprouts of corn had splintered above the surface of the soil. They moved through the crumbling dunes, smelling the smoke, and somewhere a child called out to another. The sheep headed slowly towards where a *kraal* constructed of poles and thorn bush lay against a shallow hillside.

*

When he came downstairs the sun had gone from the hallway and the dry garden beyond the back door was in shade. From the kitchen came the usual sounds of saucepans, the rattle of cutlery; a horsefly buzzed angrily against a wall. Somewhere a train blared. But these sounds did not reach Edgar Stopes as he made his way towards the front where the taproom was situated. His bath had been unsatisfactory, leaving a feeling of stickiness all over instead of coolness, and he had to wait for some time in the cramped bathroom for the motes of rust to disappear from the tepid water. He thought, hell, what a place, and to think a bloke is stuck here because of a bloody church service.

In the tiny lobby with the picture of the State President and the old hallstand, he came upon the houseboy about to sweep the front *stoep*. From the taproom came the sounds of glasses being set out.

'Hey, you,' Edgar Stopes called after the houseboy, 'Jesus Christ, I told you to bring me a beer. Hell, man, are you bloody stupid? There I was waiting and no beer. What's the matter with you, hey?'

The servant looked discomforted and made clucking sounds, fiddling with the reed broom. He said, 'Oh, master, I clean forgot. I'm sorry, I clean forgot. Mies Kroner, she gave me something to do and it clean went out of my mind.'

'Hell,' Edgar Stopes said angrily, 'And I gave you a five cent tip, too. You buggers got no appreciation.'

Sandalled feet were being rubbed nervously together. 'Master, I clean forgot.'

Edgar Stopes shook his head as if in wonder. The door from the dining-room parlour opened and Mrs. Kroner darted out, birdlike face jerking from one to the other, a table napkin clutched in a tiny claw, while she shrilled, 'What's wrong? Oh, it is you, Meneer Stopes. Anything wrong?'

Edgar Stopes scowled, 'I was only saying, I asked this *dingus* to bring me a bottle of beer, but naturally he forgot. I waited in my room for it all the time.'

'*Onnosel*, stupid,' the woman shrilled. 'You can't tell these things anything. All day I must talk to him. Can't you remember what the *baas* tells you?'

The houseboy looked shamed and Edgar Stopes said, 'Never mind now, I'll get a beer in the taproom.' He winced a little as the woman suddenly burst into screaming laughter, '*Aai*, you men with your beer.' He was going through the curtained door to the taproom, while the woman was shrilling at the servant to get on with his work and stop being so stupid.

He wiped his hot face with a clean handkerchief, the last one left, as he walked into the low, shadowy room with venetian blinds over the front window. Outside the sun was dwindling from the street, although it was still quite light. With the window-blinds and the

22

open public door, the taproom was quite cool although the electric fan suspended from the ceiling turned lazily, hardly stirring the air. The floor had been newly swept and the trough along the bottom of the bar was clean. Along one wall were two tables, and under the window a long bench. There were pictures on the walls. Above the shelf of bottles and the mirror behind the bar was a big frame of dusty gold-leaf surrounding a blow-up of an old photograph of several men posing together, some standing and others sitting near the end of a covered wagon. Most of the men were bearded and all of them wore old fashioned suits and bandoliers draped across their chests, several of them carrying rifles. The enlargement of the old print had blurred the features of the men so that they had the look of dressed-up ghosts, but Edgar Stopes knew that they were members of a commando who had fought in the Boer War. On another wall was a similarly blown-up portrait of Koos de la Rey, big beard and button-up suit. There were also two framed lithographs from the railways publicity department, of landscapes by the artist Pierneef.

Fading light that slipped through the slats of the venetian blind made dim parallels on the floor. Behind the bar stood Kroner, in shirt-sleeves wiping the top of the counter with a cloth in the immemorial gesture of all barmen. He was a square-looking man with a thick neck, reddish skin shaved close at sides and back so that the rest of his blond hair formed a stiff thatch like the roof of a *rondawel* hut, and the hands that moved on the bar were pudgy and red patterned with brown blotches. He was a big man and Stopes wondered how he had come to marry that screeching bird of a woman. Worse than Maisie, and Maisie is bad enough. Yet there was no sign of worry or submission in the blue eyes, which would have been the signs of henpecking, but instead they smiled cheerfully at him while a plump-fingered hand was extended to him over the counter.

'Well, Meneer Stopes, you are again back with us, neh? How does it go?'

The hand was damp and warm as Edgar Stopes shook it, saying, 'So so, man. Just doing the rounds and having to stop here on the way. Right now I could do with a nice cold beer.'

'What was the wife going on about?' Kroner asked, reaching under the bar for a bottle. 'I heard her going on just now.' He snapped the cap off the bottle at the gadget screwed to the wood and poured the frothing beer into a tall glass.

'Hah,' Edgar Stopes sighed with satisfaction and took a long swallow. He wiped froth from his moustache. 'I needed that. Your wife was giving the boy hell. I ordered a beer when I arrived, but the bogger didn't bring it. Had to complain. By the way, man, will you have something yourself?'

'Oh, I shall take a small lager, thanks,' the barman said. He shook his head, 'Well, you can't depend on those people. They forget things. They're not like us, you have to take them by the hand all the time, show them what to do. The wife is always having to complain. Still, there they are.' He poured his own drink and took a sip. 'How's your business then?'

'Steady,' Edgar Stopes told him. 'Once you got regular customers it's just a matter of following up, collecting orders, encouraging new products. You know how it is. How is it going here?'

'Oh, quiet. Everything is but quiet here in our little *dorp*. Nothing happens. You know about the service tomorrow?'

'Ja, I reckon I'll be staying over because the old wagon is giving a little trouble and the garage is closed tomorrow.'

The barman said, smiling with his thin mouth, 'Well, then you can mos rest up. It's nice and quiet here, no worries.'

Nice and quiet, nothing happens, Edgar Stopes thought. Sit around with a lot of bloody farmboys, a lot of bloody backward Dutchmen as dumb as the sheep they raise. Two men came into the taproom, breaking the parallels of fading sunlight as they crossed the floor. He smiled at them and they nodded back and then went to stand at the end of the bar. They wore open necked shirts, khaki shorts and laced *velskoens* dusty from the street outside. They leaned on the bar, hailing Kroner as he moved towards them and set out glasses. He did not have to hear their requests, he knew what they wanted, they belonged; but he, Edgar Stopes, was the stranger, the outsider. He thought, wiping foam from his moustache, Christ, one would think a man was a bloody nigger, them and their bloody ox-wagons and ploughs. Who's running the country, anyway? He stood at the end of the bar, alone with his beer, feeling deserted, thinking of the bright, illuminated hotel lounges at home, the throb of the juke-box, voices calling to each other the chatter about racing and the shrill voices of women with their escorts. The chatter about women brought Maisie to mind again. A damn hellcat when she'd got time, and sulky as a spoiled brat mostly. Mostly she doesn't understand, he told himself. We could get on okay together, but she doesn't understand a man just does his best. Everybody wants to get rich. It isn't my fault I'm doing this kind of work, is it? We all can't be bloody millionaires, somebody's got to peddle this junk to shopkeepers. She had started out as a good sort, but now she was a nagging thorn in the side, always going on about something or other when she had had a couple of drinks. I will have to do something, divorce maybe. Perhaps I ought to phone her, let know I'll be delayed. Why? You reckon she's waiting eagerly for you to get home? Come off it, chum. Probably sitting in some bloody flick looking at Steve McQueen and wishing it was him she was married to. But we got on all right at the beginning, it was all right then, now she was a regular bitch. He thought, The hell with them all, and motioned towards the barman.

Now he saw that the little bar-room was almost filled with men, their voices mingled in a mutter of Afrikaans, their faces red from the hard sunlight of the past days, noses peeling, lips chapped. Most of them were in shirt-sleeves and khaki trousers or shorts, and there were no women in the place because they were not allowed in bars. They also keep their women on ice, Edgar Stopes told himself. Under wraps, carefully preserved, the respected Boer woman is not for random display, much less to be seen drinking in public. Tomorrow they'll all turn out for church all right.

He thought about church because next to him two men were talking about the necessity of offering up prayers for rain, one of them saying: '... it is not natural, this drought. It is like a punishment from God. What have we done to be punished? We are a God-fearing people, is it not so?' He was a man with a broad neck, clad in a checked sports shirt, the thinning hair across the back of his head lying in lank blond strands. The thick neck was burned red above the collar, the skin coarse and flaky.

'I have put money into those sheep,' the other man said, before taking a long swallow of beer. 'Well, the *predikant*, our Dominee Visser will have something to say tomorrow. I hope he does not go on too long, I have to move the herd further to the north and it's a devil's long trek, man.'

'Well, I give that the Dominee likes a long sermon, but what he says is always sense. Let us hear what he has to say tomorrow.'

Kroner the barman came up and Edgar Stopes said, 'Brandy, a double brandy.' The man who had his back to him turned at the sound of an unfamiliar voice and looked at Edgar Stopes. He looked away again at the other man and their voices dropped, as if they were reminded that what they were discussing was very private. Edgar Stopes felt again the feeling of rejection, so that he quickly wrapped the armour of worn cynicism about himself, telling them in his mind to shove their bloody sheep and sermons because it was a lot of eye-wash, anyway.

But there was somebody else in the taproom who recognised him because a voice at his shoulder said, '*Naand*, Meneer Stopes, good evening. I took another look at your car.' It was Klaas, the red-headed man from the garage, his paunchy heaviness now shed of greasy work-clothes and draped in clean khaki shirt and trousers. His sunburned face had a scrubbed look about it, the pink scalp showing freshly through the cropped red hair. He shook his head and said, 'It is going to be a job to fix it, mister. 'I'll naturally try to do my best.'

Edgar Stopes said, 'Well, just so I can get home. It's only a couple of hours to the city, half a day at most. I will -ah-appreciate, consider it a big service, if you can fix it so I can make it to the city.'

'Well, I can't promise you nothing, hey. We will have to see. But you should take it in for a thorough overhaul when you get home.' He took a swallow from the glass he held in one huge hand. 'I will work on it tomorrow afternoon, I'll work on it awright.'

Before he could say anything further there were men at his side, tugging at his sleeves, laughing and one of them saying, '*Kom aan*, Klaas, there's Dirk Nels who boasts that he can beat you at finger-pulling. Come on, we have bet a round on you. That Dirky, he reckons he can pull you open in two minutes.' The red-haired man laughed, showing his yellow teeth, and turned away from Edgar Stopes with the others.

One part of the taproom had been cleared and two chairs set facing each other. One of the chairs was occupied by a fat man with a ruddy moonface and shaven head. His massive shoulders hunched over his belly as he sat with his great hands on his knees, smiling at the men gathered around, looking up with a jovial greeting as Klaas and the other men pushed their way up. Edgar Stopes made his way towards the scene, drinking from his glass, the brandy warming his insides, spreading a feeling of heartiness, of public relations again. Men were pushing the red-haired man into the second chair, patting his great shoulders, and the two contenders clasped mighty hands in greeting.

'*Ek sê*, Klaas, I say, man, are you ready for a little struggle?'

The red-haired man smiled, 'Just as you say, Nels, just as you say.'

'Well, you beat that *outjie* from Maritzdorp last year at the games, hey,' the fat man said, smiling back. 'I reckon I got a little more weight than he had.'

'Weight, ja, but weight isn't everything, *ou kêrel*.'

'Well, let us get on with it then. Somebody will have to pay for a round of beer.'

One hand pressed on a thigh, forearms of the other held rigid while their forefingers locked, the tug-of-war between the two hefty men commenced and the onlookers crowded around, calling encouragement. Edgar Stopes found himself being jostled aside, and tried for a few minutes to see what was going on over the heads of the men crowded about the straining contestants. Then he withdrew from the scene with assumed indifference, making his way back to the bar, thinking, like bloody kids they are, like bloody kids.

Back at the bar a tall and good-looking, fair-haired man was saying to Kroner: ' . . . that Nels was always a man to stand fast. I remember one time at the country games when he took on all comers.' This man was tall and carried himself like a rugby-forward, and wore his neat slacks and light windbreaker with the ease of one born to informality. He had a smooth, handsome, cheerful-looking face, the eyes clear, the teeth even and white as he smiled aside at Edgar Stopes who was leaning on the bar beside him.

'Ah, a visitor to our little dorp?' the handsome man said, and Edgar Stopes recognised the tone at once. Another one after goodwill, eager for friendly public relations. He's wondering what I'm doing here, whether I can be of use to him. I wonder what *he's* trying to sell. Experience of competing with rival salesmen had taught him to suspect another's cheerful approaches, to see behind the disarming smile, the slap on the back. But this man was a local and could not be concerned with laying on the virtues of Smilebrite toothbrushes or a new line of egg-beaters.

Edgar Stopes smiled back, nodding and Kroner was saying to him against the background of voices from the finger-pulling contest, 'This is Meneer Meulen, Meneer Hannes Meulen. Meneer Meulen is going to be our candidate in the elections for the Volksraad.'

Ah, thought Edgar Stopes, that's what he's going to sell to these country bumpkins, and he said, extending a hand, 'Well, it's a pleasure, sir. Stopes, is my name. I wish you luck, really.' His hand was taken in a hard grip while the clear eyes smiled on, the white teeth flashing, and Meulen was saying, *'Dankie.'*

'What'll you have?' Stopes asked.

'Well, I will only take a beer, thanks.' Meulen said, and Stopes was glad to hear that he accepted without a sense of superiority. This was no competition he must be thinking, Stopes imagined. Here today and gone tomorrow and no arguments about who is offering the better value in plastic cups.

Kroner said, drawing the beer, 'Mister Stopes, he keeps the dorp in supplies. Sees to it that all our shops are always stocked up.'

Behind them the finger-pulling match was going on amid cries of excitement, and Meulen said, 'Yes, it is needful to keep in touch with the countryfolk, Mister Stopes. You are lucky in that your affairs bring you among us. I am really talking of contact between the English-speaking people and the Afrikaans. In these times it is necessary that we stand together.'

Edgar Stopes, with beer suds on his moustache said, 'I agree, one hundred per cent.'

The handsome man asked, 'Are you of any party, Meneer Stopes?'

'Well, ah, not really,' Edgar Stopes replied. 'In my line of business ... '

'I understand altogether. But parties need not divide us. What must be uppermost in our minds must be the survival of our united people. We live in dangerous times. If you read what is going on ...'

'Hoor, hoor,' said Kroner, nodding his thatched head in the background.

'... All the more reason why we must forget old wounds and think of the common good. I am talking about our way of life, everything which our people have done to make this a hospitable and proud country.'

'Well, I'm with you there. man,' Edgar Stopes said. 'I myself am not a political man, hear, but I do wish you the best of *geluk*.'

'Are you staying with us for a little time?'

'My car is at the garage, being —ah— made right, mended,' Edgar Stopes said. 'I reckon I shall be here for all of tomorrow.'

'Well, maybe we will get a chance to talk some more,' Meulen said wiping his lips with a snowy handkerchief. 'I'm staying here at

Kroner's too, until after the church service. We will meet, I am sure. Dankie for the beer.'

'No thanks necessary,'

The handsome face and white teeth smiled at him and then Meulen was saying to Kroner, 'If anybody needs me, say that I've gone to the Steen house.' He sauntered over to the finger-pulling contest which was still without result, and Edgar Stopes saw the men turning towards him, nodding, smiling, shaking the hand of their parliamentary candidate.

Kroner was saying, 'Meneer Meulen owns one of the sheep farms around here. That is to say, his oupa, grandfather, owns it but it is really Hannes who runs it. The old man is past his time for such affairs.' He gestured with a thumb towards the blurred blow-up of the Boer War commando. 'That's Oupa Johannes Meulen there. Left home as a young man, just a lad, to ride with de la Rey. When he came back after the war the British could have shot him as a traitor, but they left him alone, did nothing.'

Edgar Stopes peered at the picture but saw only the group of figures with unidentifiable faces, some bearded, all anonymous, posing with their bandoliers and Mauser rifles. He looked again to where Hannes Meulen was watching the contest, laughing with the other men, and thought, bit of a pompous ass, if you ask me. English and Afrikaans people unite — but did he bother to speak a bit of English? Not him. Stopes found that his first impression of Meulen had to be amended.

Kroner was saying, thick mottled arms on the bar, 'Ja, a good man to represent this region. He has our people at heart. Some years ago there was trouble with a kaffir and he got a suspended sentence, but it was really a small matter and nobody around here thinks about it. A good man, ja, and he will get on in this country.'

Outside the daylight was finally receding leaving the bar-room in shadow. Edgar Stopes thought he might as well go and try some of Mrs Kroner's spiced and skewered chops. He finished what was in his glass, waved a hand at the barman and made his way towards the glass doors. Behind him the finger-pulling match broke up amid cheers, laughter, and thigh-slapping, but he did not bother to find out who the victor was.

★

A long time ago it had been the perpetual scene of mine dumps and the grease-stained and rusty remains of machinery, the dark skeletons of disused mineheads. Beyond all that you came into the untidy old streets, the shabby hotels with iron balconies, rows of one storey cottages. After the big strike the white miners who lived there had trickled away, but her father had stayed on, as if it would have been an act of indecency to abandon the little shop with its barricades of tins of jam, the sharp-smelling bars of washing soap, the ranked bottles of cooking oil.

The artillery of the government, the rifles, shot-guns and sticks of dynamite of the defeated miners had passed into history books, but the little shop still stood. Her father had sometimes pointed out the old bullet holes in the wall outside, as if he had actually taken part in the fighting. But he had actually locked up the place and, safe upstairs in the tiny flat, he had peeped bravely through the gap in the window shutter while his wife had crouched terrified by the wardrobe.

Afterwards he would remark with pride that he'd seen it all, or that he'd even taken part, gone through it all. Sometimes he lied and claimed he'd known Taffy Long. The fact of the matter was that at that time he had recently bought the little store, lock, stock, and barrel, from the estate of an old Syrian who had passed on, and since he had nothing to do with strikes and miners and the bloody government, what the hell was there to be scared of? Why should he not stay?

Gradually the Whites drifted away from the area to settle in other spots, but Barends stuck, even though the coolies and coloureds and the bloody Chinamen moved in to surround them. They had to eat too, didn't they? They needed condensed milk and curry powder and hair-nets, didn't they?

But it was not really the same. A man couldn't get into proper conversation with the population. What could you talk to a damn applesammy about? When his wife died of something to do with her bowels, Barends seemed to surrender completely and he began to care less about the shop. The years passed. The stacked products gathered dust — he wasn't selling well because on top of it all there were coolie shops around too. The old barricades of canned and bottled goods became lost under strewn scraps of paper, empty cartons carelessly stacked; the cheese got mixed up with soap; the tobacco with the tins of sardines. It was like fortifications left to crumble after a war. Upstairs the little flat grew shabbier and the sherry bottles began to gather on the untidy sideboard.

'You've got to pull your socks up, man,' his brother admonished whenever he visited. His brother worked on the railways. He had started as a shunter when the government had decided to replace Black workers more and more with Whites. They called it Civilised Labour. Later he'd become a ganger and now was a foreman. 'Time's passing, things are looking up, and here you are wasting away in this godforsaken place. Look at all these bloody coolies and coons around you, why, *they* seem even better off.'

'Well, at least I'm in business, aren't I?'

'Ach, business is all very well, but this one is going to the dogs. I tell you what, you need to marry again, man. True as God, that's the thing old man.'

It was his brother who introduced him to Elizabeth Gray. The three of them spent a few evenings in a hotel lounge, chatting idly. She wore big dentures that seemed to clatter when she talked. Her husband had died of phthisis, she was lonely too, but in a different way. A formidable woman, with red hair and a face like a limestone crag, she needed things to regulate, people to dominate. Before he knew it, Barends was swept up along with his shop.

Business picked up, everything became spick and span, severely orderly, under her firm, almost grim direction, and they thrived even in that area. Most of the groceries disappeared — they could be purchased elsewhere — to be replaced by bottles of soft drinks; magazines appeared, comic papers, pulp novels, most of the daily newspapers, even those which started catering for the Blacks, film and fashion magazines. In addition there were other little knick-knacks needed by any household: tea strainers and cutlery, can openers, brush-and-comb sets — the little coolie grocers did not specialise in such things. A succession of Indian lads was hired to do the cleaning up and other odd jobs. A fat black woman came once a week to dust and polish and take away bundles of washing. For the rest, everything was run by the former widow, now Missus Elizabeth Barends. She ordered stock and arranged displays, rang the till and made up the books, while her husband faded more and more into the background, or rather spent most of his time upstairs. He became like some shade haunting the premises, the traditional ghost that went with the castle; a little, withdrawn man more like a hanger-on around the store than anybody to do with ownership.

So it might have come as a surprise to him, as it was to everybody else — most of the friends were his wife's — when the daughter was born. It was as if his wife had timed and ordered the conception too, like arranging the delivery of a side of veal.

'We'll call her Maisie,' his wife said in the hospital bed. 'That's a nice name.' Barends wondered why, but did not disagree, sitting humbly at the bedside, with the packet of bananas and the box of assorted biscuits he had brought her held awkwardly on his lap. A child after all these years, and the event frightened him. He was getting on, and Lizzie — if one might say so — was no chicken, though she bore her Amazonian figure well.

The War passed, then there was a strike by the black miners and Barends remembered the old days. But it didn't come this way and he read the newspaper accounts. It wasn't the same, and though the soldiers and police had been turned out with fixed bayonets the blacks did not have the shot-guns and dynamite as in those times. They could be handled and the police had rounded up a lot of Communists.

'I'm not interested in politics,' his new wife said. 'That's awright for the government and the kaffirs. There's the business to see to.'

The child was kept upstairs, among the fairly new modernistic furniture — the sideboard and the old wardrobe where the first Mrs Barends had cowered had all gone — because all the children in the neighbourhood were a lot of coons. When the time came for her to go to school Barends escorted her to the distant White school, taking her there in the morning and fetching her in the afternoon, travelling on the segregated tramcars. After school she could be with her mother in the shop. Her father showed her the old bullet holes. For the most part she watched the till being rung as her mother served the dark people who came in or read comic books, paged through the film and fashion magazines, drank bottles of pop. She did not complete high school; primary had been passable, but high proved a bore so she became inattentive and failed the examinations.

'She'll be a help in the shop,' Mrs Barends said. 'It's not such a hard job giving change, even though arithmetic ain't her best subject.'

It wasn't so bad helping in the shop. In between counting money she could sit and read the film magazines or look at the latest fashions in the girls' clothes. But it could be a bore too. Luckily the shop closed Saturday afternoons and she went to the bioscope, the one for Europeans Only. She knew the histories of most of the film stars, especially the males; and she had her hair done in the styles the female ones introduced. One week she was Alice Faye or June Allyson, another she was Greer Garson or Alexis Smith, Lana Turner.

Upstairs in the tiny cramped room that was hers she would gaze at herself in the wardrobe mirror, considered her bare body from all angles. Jesus, that's me! Long ago she had discovered her breasts. I think I look a little like Rhonda Fleming, she thought.

Beyond the chintz-curtained windows the rusting corrugated roofs and cracked parapets of the slum stretched away to the rectangular skyscrapers of the city centre. The segregated tram-cars clang-clanged in the distance.

'God,' her mother scolded sometimes. 'Don't you think of anything else but bioscope and blerry film actresses? We've got a business to run, and it's for your benefit. You'll have it when we're gone.'

'What's so wonderful about this?' Maisie would venture to retort petulantly. 'Serving a lot of niggers.' She imagined the bright lights, the flashing neon signs of the city centre.

'You got no 'preciation, like your pa.'

Past the shop windows the dark people went by outside and there was a perpetual smell of oriental spices in the air.

There were boys now and then, men in the foyers of cinemas. But petting in the dark auditorium depended on what film hero the particular choice resembled. There would be Tony Curtis, but soon the Tony Curtis hairstyle became too common. That one looked a little like Alan Ladd, that one like Audie Murphy.

There was always a pound or two sneaked from the till on Saturdays, so after the matinée there would be the milkbars, the hot-dog counters, secret cigarettes, the daring gins and lime, breath disguised with peppermint on the way home after dark, often too late for her mother's satisfaction.

Once a gang of them, boys and girls, went on a wild drive around in a car. Tangled legs and groping hands, playful giggling, and the boys in pomaded hair with ducktail coiffures produced bottles of wine and there was a funny smell mingled with that of their hand-rolled cigarettes. She remembered they all landed up at the Zoo Lake in the dark, the laughing, the shrieking; sometime or other too drunk and reckless with the partner she'd chosen — she thought he looked a little like Robert Mitchum. 'Hey, don't get funny, hey.' Afterwards, straightening up her dishevelment on the way back, she'd got them to drop her off near home. Back in her room she'd examined herself in the mirror, feeling a little anxious. Nothing seemed to show, and thank God nothing came of it. No more outings like that she vowed.

'We'll have to keep you in hand, young lady,' more than once snapped the large and looming Mrs Barends, clashing her dentures. 'In future it'll be straight home from the pitchers for you. One night the kaffirs will get you, you'll see. If there was any pertickler young man, there's no need to be afraid of bringing him here for us to have a look at, like any respectable girl.' *We* was a sort of Royal pronoun, it did not really include the subdued ageing ghost who shared the place.

God, how could she bring any fellow home? Right on the edge of coolieland? During the day the white sherry tramps drank from bottles in alleyways, Indian women in saris jabbered on the pavements. She usually came alone on the tramcar that stopped a little distance away, running the few blocks, so the boys really didn't have to see where she lived.

Then came the time Edgar Stopes made his appearance. The regular salesman came in one afternoon and said cheerfully, 'Afternoon folks, I want you to meet my colleague who's taking over my round. This here's Edgar, Edgar Stopes, he'll give you the same good service I'm sure you know I been giving.'

He looks a little like Van Johnson, Maisie Barends thought from behind the magazine rack. Or perhaps Brian Donlevy, maybe a mixture of both. She came forward and the new young salesman shook hands with mother and daughter, smiling broadly: show the customer you're always happy to meet them. This dolly wasn't too bad, red-blonde and busty. The father was upstairs, listening to Springbok Radio.

So there he was coming in regularly each month to fill in the order book so Missus Barends could top up the supplies of the shop. 'Nice little business you got here, ladies,' he smiled, licking the point of his pencil. 'A good business, that's the thing I always say. Money in the till, money in the bank. You've got to have it *here* to run a nice place like this.' He tapped his dark blond hair with the pencil. 'In God we trust and all others cash, that's my motto.'

'That young man has got *go*,' Elizabeth Barends said sometime later. 'That's what I like in a man — go.' He'll get *places*, you'll see. Not like that father of yours.'

'You mean going from shop to shop taking orders?' Maisie asked with pronounced scepticism.

'You got no eye for the future,' her mother clattered. 'Like your father. Why, I remember the state this place was in when I came along — just another coolie shop. What I mean is, is that Stopes will advance beyond just taking orders. Manager or something.'

With an eye on the nubile Maisie, Edgar Stopes one day ventured to treat the whole family to an evening at the lounge of one of the hotels in town. 'Hell,' he said jovially, 'You can't *just* look after the shop. All work and no play et cetera, you know.' It was an investment for the future: Maisie looked a bit of a good thing, but he had to tolerate the vast woman and old Boris Karloff.

'Well I reckon it'll be awright,' Missus Barends clattered, which was the sound that accompanied excitement or her rare smiles 'S'pose a night off wouldn't be so bad. But of course, our Maisie isn't a drinker though.'

'Oh, we'll carry her home,' Stopes chuckled.

They had a table in the noisy lounge that was lighted with blue-shaded lamps. The old girl's limestone face looked ghastly in the subdued blue glow while she daintily sipped her ginger-square. The father crouched meekly over his lager, and Edgar Stopes thought, 'Jesus, what a lot.' He drank whisky and nudged Maisie's knee with his and she smiled slightly at him over the shandy the old girl had allowed her. They didn't know about the secret gins and lime. She was a good-looker, Stopes thought, though she's got funny sort of eyes, like green stones. After a while he managed to hold one of her hands out of sight under the table and delicately tickled the palm, while he pretended to be interested in something the terrible mother was saying.

Once when Maisie was alone in the shop, he said seriously, 'Listen, a good-looking dolly like you don't belong in a place like this ... standing behind the counter. You ought to get out, go places. I mean with a bloke.'

'Oh, I go places,' she told him, looking at him with her cold green eyes. 'Don't think I'm stuck *here* all the time. There *are* chaps I know.'

He laughed, 'I reckon there are. But I tell you what, if I ask the old lady to take you out one Saturday night on our own and she agrees, will you go?'

'Where'd we go? Bioscope? A caffy? The lounge?'

'Lounge,' he said with a friendly sarcasm: 'You can go *there* any time. We'll go dancing, maybe the Country Club. A posh enough place, just where you belong.' He winked an eye at her. 'What d'you say, hey?'

'Country Club? You a member?'

'Member? Well, sure, man. Otherwise I wouldn't invite you, would I?'

'Well, I'll kind of think about it. Here's the order my mum left ... she had to go see some relation.' Before leaving he noticed that her hair was then a pale blond colour.

'I don't mind,' Missus Barends said, showing the dentures like miniature tombstones, 'As long as you look after my little girl.'

'Ha, ha, you can rely on me,' Edgar Stopes chuckled. It was a few weeks later and he was scribbling an order in his book. 'It'll be a pleasure to escort the delightful Miss Barends.' He ran a surreptitious eye over the healthy bustline, then asked: 'Business okay?'

'Getting on awright. This is a steady thing, you know, hey.'

'It is, it is. You sell the things people need and keep the customers happy, that's the thing. But don't let 'em get the upper hand. You can't afford to do any favours. Like credit for instance.' He shut his order book and snapped the elastic band around it. 'People don't appreciate favours. Look at those stupid natives, refusing to ride their bloody buses — begging your pardon. They got their own buses and then they go an' boycott them because of fares. We all got to pay fares. So what do they get as a result? Sore feet.'

'Well, they are kind of poor, aren't they?' Maisie said, looking up from the cover of a magazine. 'The fares went up, it said so in the papers.'

Stopes shrugged. 'Poor; there's no need to be poor. Are you poor, am I poor? No, because we got initiative, hey. We got *brains*. Look after number one, that's what I say. If it wasn't for people like us, why the country would never be civilised. Who wants sore feet?' He patted her hand playfully. 'Not *you*, because I've got a car, that's the thing.'

'He seems a decent sort of fellow,' Missus Barends mused while she stacked the Wrigley's chewing-gum. 'He's got go-ahead. Just think, at his age he's awready made plans for the future. While we was chatting the other night at the lounge, he was saying he's awready taken out life insurance. Just think, providing for his future wife in her old age.'

'God, what'll I *wear*?' Maisie moaned. 'Who cares about insurance and all that. I haven't got a decent dress, specially for a country club.' Christ, she thought, just to get out of this blerry place.

'Oh, we'll go into town Saturday morning and look at some things. I think your father will manage for the morning, providing he pays attention and don't let that little sammy, Ismail, steal half the damn coconut balls. Just think, when *he* dies of old age or accident or something, *his* wife'll be well off. An' there's a pension scheme with his firm too, for his retirement. Now, we'll pick up something nice; maybe we'll even go to one of the high-class shops.'

When Edgar Stopes called in his Chevrolet, there she was all dressed to the T. The orange mouth smiled boldly, but somehow it didn't match the bleached but carefully dressed hair, yet the frock she wore emphasised the young hips and that horrible mother of hers had even allowed a bit of upper tit to show. Edgar Stopes was pleased. He thought anticipatorily, I bet you she's a virgin too.

They drove away from the dreary district through the traffic-crowded canyons of the city, the huge granite cliffs of office blocks, hotels and apartment houses brilliant with neon signs and rolling lights. The pavements were crowded and around the theatre marquees there were expensive people. Maisie gazed out at Life, while Edgar said, 'I'm changing this bus for a new one. The firm gives you an allowance.' His order book still lay in the open cubby-hole.

The Country Club sprawled beyond the other end of the city, amid parkland and trees. The car park was hung with coloured lights and from inside the building a band played samba music. In the entrance hall Stopes made her go to the Ladies to fix her hair, while he arranged for the table, he said. The fact of the matter was that he wanted her out of the way so she didn't notice he had to pay the extra visitor's entrance fee because he was not a member of the club, contrary to what he had told her. Then a ballroom with tables around the sides, more coloured lights and Chinese lanterns, Jerry's Stompers on the stage decorated with gold and silver tinsel, a terrace outside a glass doorway, while a waiter showed them to a table.

'Like it?' Edgar Stopes asked after he'd ordered a gin and lime for her and a brandy for himself from the Indian waiter who wore a red peajacket and white gloves.

'Mmmm, I've never been to a place like this before.' But, she thought, it's not like those places on the movies: Rita Hayworth, Gene Kelly.

'You're too cooped up, deary,' he said over the drinks. 'Jussus, stuck in that shop selling stuff to a lot of darkies, You deserve better.'

'You reckon so, really?'

'I'm telling you, ain't I? You got to look ahead. That gin and lime awright?'

'Mmmm, thanks.' She shrugged her bare shoulders. 'Well, what can a girl do? That's life, I reckon.'

He ordered more drinks. 'There, you see? Your attitude, it's not right. You got to get after the gravy, everybody for himself and the devil take the bugger at the back. *That's* life.'

'What's it *you're* after, mister smart guy?' She peered at him with mock scepticism in the green eyes.

He chuckled and winked knowingly. 'You want to dance?'

They went onto the floor and jostled among the rest of the couples. She said against his shoulder, 'So you think poor little me deserves better, do you?' The gins and limes made her feel gay.

'Well, what I mean is, you ought to get out more.'

'That's all then?'

He tickled her back and pressed a thigh against hers and she said, 'Naughty, naughty. I know what *you* mean by the gravy.'

After another drink he said, 'This place is getting noisy as hell, let's go outside. You haven't seen the rest of the club.'

'What's outside?'

'Well, I want to show you, isn't it?'

She let him lead her among the noisy tables and out through the glass doorway. The terrace was strung with more coloured lights, like Christmas decorations the management had forgotten to take down, dusty, cheap and tawdry. Beyond the terrace were tennis courts, a swimming pool, golf-links, more grass and trees. He had a hand fiddling with her hip and he said tentatively, 'We could go for a stroll.'

'Where, out there? What else is there to see?'

'See? Well, I meant just a stroll like. A walk.'

Smiling at him with the orange mouth and the cold green eyes. 'Naughty, naughty, hey? Think I can't take my gin an' limes, hey? You can't catch me out like that, outjie.'

He said, finding himself flushing, 'Hell, Maisie, I'm not that kind of chap, you ought to know.'

'Give Maisie another cigarette. How do I ought to know? Our first night out and how do I ought to know?' She smiled at him, the orange mouth passionless, sly.

He said grinning, 'Well, I kind of go for you, Maisie. The first time I saw you I reckoned, that's the girl for me.'

'That's not the first time any girl's been told that, Mister Edgar Stopes.'

'No, I reckon not. But really, Maisie . . .'

Behind them the band played the twist, She stared out into the gloom with her agate eyes: at the golf-links, the tennis court, the dark line of trees like waiting dragons, and remembered the Zoo Lake, dishevelment, the rough first copulation.

He said, probing: 'Well, if you kind of don't want to stay we could go to my place for a drink.'

The girl on the screen in the old routine. She had thoughts of a tall apartment block, a modern bachelor flat, but he wasn't bloody Cary Grant after all, only a salesman, with a future maybe. Yet the alternative was that great meal-bag of a woman with the clashing teeth of a movie dinosaur. 'My place' was a flat down a flagstone pathway across a rough, narrow lawn behind a bungalow. The flat was really an outhouse, separate from the main building; perhaps it had once been servants' quarters, but now it was cluttered with the odds and ends bachelors accumulated and a modern-looking drinks cabinet with a coffee table scarred with cigarette-burns in front of it; a picture of *voortrekkers* that must have come with the place . . . she couldn't imagine him buying a print of ox-wagons crossing the veld. But another section was the bed alcove, cramped, untidy, the bed unmade, scattered with soiled clothes, strewn socks. He produced more gin and lime — perhaps he had prepared for this. Later she heard herself in the crook of his arm, as if somebody else spoke, somebody exotic: You'll be kind to me, won't you?'

But he had a small, irksome feeling that it was not he who was the victor.

Missus Barends did not mind them going out together regularly. After all it was about time Maisie had a steady boyfriend, somebody to look after her, assume responsibility, and Edgar had ambition, drive, he'd get places: from local salesman to district representative, manager, perhaps one day a company director. Edgar had other ideas: he had something going steady on the side with this dolly who was full of ideas about glamour and bright lights, and she was enthusiastic enough, although sometimes her frenzy startled him. Keep the customers satisfied, he thought happily.

But there she was, sitting across the seat of the car from him, in the shabby, darkened street outside the shop shut up for the night, saying, 'What you going to do about it? I'm sure I'm in the family way.'

Oh Jesus, he thought, oh Jesus. Then he remembered something and said, 'Hell, how can you say that? We were careful, wasn't we?'

'Careful, careful,' she snapped. 'How can a person be careful all the time?'

'What'll we do then?' he asked and it sounded like a moan.

'Well, what d'you think we going to do, hey? What's the old woman going to say when she finds out? There'll be complaints to your boss — you don't know *her*.'

'Oh, hell.'

She said, 'What do you mean, oh hell? I thought we was going steady, we was thinking ahead like. What's so suddenly serious if it happens now or after we was married? All it needs is for us to get married *soon*.'

He mumbled, 'Well . . . well . . . Jesus, Maisie.'

Smiling at him with the mouth that was not bright pink, but the eyes were the same cold green baubles, mimicking him: '*You've got to go after the gravy. Every man for himself.* So I'm the bladdy gravy, am I? *You're too cooped up, dreary, standing in that shop and serving a lot of darkies.*' She looked petulant now. 'You think I want to go on living in this godforsaken shop? You think I enjoy serving those coons day after day? I want to get on too, don't I? I thought you and me was going to get married, and I didn't mind getting like this if it was by you. Why, I always thought sort-of about a chap like you coming along, to get me away from that bladdy shop and away from that great big cow of an old woman and that wrinkled up old man of mine. And now you want to go and let me down and all.'

Missus Barends wondered why they were in such a hurry to get married. Her first thought was, of course, that Maisie had gone and got herself into trouble, but her daughter assured her crossly it was not like that at all. It was that Edgar anticipated some sort of promotion and transfer somewhere else and they had thought they'd get married before all these changes came and all that. There was Edgar agreeing. They had to look ahead, not let the grass grow under their feet, start on the new road together.

That was all very well, the mother agreed. It was a good attitude, but she was still suspicious. However, her suspicions proved unfounded, for months after the wedding there was no sign of Maisie's pregnancy.

'If you people wasn't in such a hurry we could of had a proper do and maybe a picture of you two in the *Women's Mail*,' she grumbled, which for once did not produce the clattering.

Edgar Stopes transferred to another area after a time, but there was no indication of the talked-of promotion either. He and Maisie seemed to get on as a married couple, but it was not what Edgar Stopes had meant to happen at all.

★

They came down to where houses had come to rest in a bend in the bank of the dry stream bed. Here there were still leaves on the trees that grew hunched and crookedly patterned against the sky that was turning mauve with twilight; the houses were broken up into groups near the trees to squat in the shade they threw when the sun was high. Some of the houses were of the old circular style with thatched roofs; but in the main they were straight-walled, built as the old huts had crumbled away, some of the walls mud and branch-poles, with designs scratched in the plaster when it had still been wet. There were gardens here and there, but the vegetation had dwindled and their walls fallen in places, as if the dying plant life had infected the brown clay. In hollow yards outdoor ovens sent up columns of smoke and the children tended them now, nursing the fires while the elders headed towards the open space in front of Hlangeni's house.

Along the pathways, dust drifted like a fog and clung to the German-print dresses of the older women, powdered the coats of the dogs twitching in the shadows, and settled in new layers on the rusty roofs. At one end of the village a group of children with buckets, saucepans, and containers, waited under a tree for the wagon which would bring drums of water from the railway station.

The one who was called Shilling Murile noted that many of the houses had been put up after he had left and that long remembered things had disappeared. Most of the outside ovens had gone and now there were more cookers inside, kitchen tables, saucepans. Eight years had brought changes, he told himself. It was as if rage had always been there, like the scarred knees of childhood, the horniness of feet from years barefoot in the gritty soil. But his rage was a personal thing, keeping him away from these people who

41

were now almost like strangers to him, so that he led the way around the outskirts of the village, through ruined huts and fallen thatched roofs, as if meeting somebody he knew from years' ago might spoil the savour of hatred.

The shepherd pattered after him in the dwindling light of the day, tattered blanket flapping, saying, 'If it's going to be a long *indaba*, a lengthy discourse, one should have one's pipe well filled. A pipe helps a man to listen, to ponder.'

Madonele the shepherd was anxious not to lose this source of good tobacco. Without money it was impossible to get tobacco and the trader had long ago ceased to give credit to those who had no income from relations working in the cities. Undoubtedly this young man was somewhat strange, but one could not help being affected a little after so many years ago, when the Murile boys had caused consternation in the village with their pranks. But now he was strange, distant, perhaps really a ghost of the past. He was happy to hear Murile say, not unkindly but with a dryness of voice, 'You will have your tobacco, old one.'

They moved together in the general direction of the meeting place and once the young man paused at the sound of children's voices coming from around the oven mound in the yard beyond a tumbled wall. Perhaps he remembered something from the past: a girl's giggle, tight-plaited hair, the sight of a wash-faded frock, the grey knees as the children hunched around the old ashes, the frayed khaki shorts, the riddles of long ago.

'There is a woman who has many children and they are to be seen covering a great plain with the mother in their midst. Ah, but whenever the husband approaches, she and her children run and hide away.'

'Why, that is easy. You mean the moon, the stars and the sun.'

'What is the white-necked raven?'

'The white-necked raven is a missionary.'

'Why?'

'Surely because he wears a white collar and a black coat. You see, I know the birds.'

'Do you know the butcherbird?'

'Yes, I know the butcherbird. That he is a hunter and smeller-out of sorcerers, because he impales insects.'

The shepherd said, sounding a little anxious, 'We should not be late, brother.'

42

'Listen, madala,' the other said, looking a little surly, 'I did not come for any indaba. I came because I lived here once, came out of a desire to look on things I once saw, before going my way. It is not for Hlangeni's speeches that I came.'

'Where will you go?' the shepherd asked, a~ they went on along the ridge below which the villagers were gathering.

The one called Shilling Murile shrugged. 'Who knows? I do not care, after I have done what has to be done.'

'What will you do?'

'You are a talkative old man, as bad as a chief.' He smiled bitterly, a fleeting twist of the mouth, and was serious again, kicking at the dust with the thick-soled boots, his hands clenched in the pockets of his trousers, the old army blouse pulled tight across his heavy shoulders, looking down to where the villagers were meeting.

The people had gathered in the dusty patch of ground that fronted Hlangeni's house. The house stood a little above the others, on a rise shaded by old blue-gum trees, and it had a stoep revetted with packed stones that had started to come loose in places. Once a wall had surrounded the yard in front of the house, but the mud had cracked and crumbled and now there were only sections standing, and the yard gate was gone. But this was still the chief's house and so there was quiet as the crowd gathered, most of them moving under the trees that came down into the yard. There were mostly women in the crowd with young boys and older men who squatted towards the front and when Hlangeni came out onto the stoep there was a noise of greeting.

He came out into the warm shade with the two who were his councillors: he was a dwindling old man in a dusty black suit in spite of the heat, an old fashioned collar, and a wrinkled necktie. Once Hlangeni had had square shoulders as befitted his square body, but of late the shoulders had sagged and shrunk and he had a crumpled look. The broad face had caved in so that the dark folds which had once been crags were now loose as landslides, and his hair had gone whiter so that he wore a cap of snow. It was as if he was slowly slipping away to eventually disappear into the old black suit. All this had started when the government had arbitrarily demoted him from chief to a mere headman; and although his people still recognised him as chief, the decree of white officialdom had commenced to wither him so that now he stood awkward and unsure in the shade, surrounded by doubt, trying to clasp at the cloak of old dignity that was wearing thin. His brown eyes, dry as old leaves, peered out into the sunlight and he thought morosely 'I have become a chief of women.' The thought frightened him and he tried to force his mind back to another time, far-off youth, when he had dreamed of warriors.

But one of the men with him was whispering, 'It is time,' and he looked with surprise at this man, asking, 'Are you not going to say anything first, Kobe?'

The man Kobe looked away. He was the one who had to introduce the chief, to praise him before the gathering each time he appeared. He was the public reciter, but now he did not feel like eulogising this frightened old man. So he merely said, addressing the crowd: 'Here is Hlangeni who is your chief.' He added simply, 'We have seen the magistrate again, and he said that the order is final, that we shall have to move.'

Hlangeni thought, it is no longer like the old times when a chief had power, authority; when a chief's praises were sung in a loud voice. This thought produced a twinge of pride, so that he spoke aloud, startled by the sound of his own voice, saying: 'The sun is going to his rest. See, the day ends. Is one day like another?' He gestured with a black sleeve towards the west where the fading day blazed in orange, pink and gold along the horizon beyond the village.

'Is one day like another? There was a day when all this was our land. Here we planted crops and raised sheep as our fathers did before us and their fathers before them. On that hill our ancestors are buried. Here our young men and girls danced. There were good days and bad days, fat years and lean years. When the time was good there were many children and fat lambs, grass and corn, beautiful beadwork and happy songs. When the time was bad we weathered it and our ancestors were always with us. Good times or bad times, fat days or lean days, here was our home. The evil times were our times as were the good. But now there is an evil that is not ours.

'The evil that comes from the white man is not ours. The evil that comes from his laws and guns and money is not ours. The white man says that his laws are made for all, but the laws are his, not ours. The white men took our young men from us to work for them and we watched it being done knowing that the law was the white man's law. Our fields and our cattle could not be tended because our men are needed for those of the whites, that their harvests might grow abundant and their cattle grow fat. That is according to their law, not ours.

'Now their law has said that this is no longer our land, our home, that it is needed by the whites, and that is according to their law, not ours. But their law is made for all they say, and we must obey. Once all these parts were our land. Then the whites came and defeated our ancestors and took most of the land, leaving us this. Here is our land and the land of our ancestors since those times when they first came. This has been our earth and soil and our home since those times. Now they have put a mark on our doors and have said, You must go. A door opens to a man's home. Is it such a terrible thing to love one's home? But their law was made for all, they say, even if it is not our law.

'It is bitterly known that their laws and weapons make all brotherhood impossible, that they can penetrate and destroy even manhood. So we must bow our heads before this and our people must kneel and sink even as the sun sets upon another day.'

His voice faltered and he stood silent, looking a little shamed, as if he had withdrawn a little more into the shabby black suit, pride slipped away. There was a stillness in the crowd except for a cough here and there, the shuffle of feet in the dust of the yard. Somewhere a dog barked. Then the crowd moved, swayed, was split apart and a voice boomed from it. 'What a song,' the voice boomed. 'A song fit to be sung at funerals.'

The woman who spoke thrust her way through the people while she shouted: 'Bah, the sun will come up again tomorrow.'

From the shade at the front of his house Hlangeni said, 'Woman, sister, you have no right . . .'

'Right?' Is this not a meeting of the village? I shall speak.'

Beside him Hlangeni heard the man, Kobe, say, 'Let her speak. Besides, she's your own sister.'

Below them the woman was going on: 'All this business about the sun. So the sun sets and the sun rises. Do we have to weep over that? People are born and people die, but there are always people.' She was Hlangeni's sister, and while he dwindled away it seemed as if she grew. A heavy square woman, she looked as if she had been constructed out of blocks of dark wood of various sizes, the uppermost of which had been roughly carved with eye-sockets, nose, nostrils, cheekbones, a great gash of a mouth, and then sanded and polished to a shiny smoothness. She wore a dusty headcloth, a vast dress like a tent strapped around the middle with an old leather belt, and on her feet a man's boots, cracked and down-at-heel. She brandished a hand like a spade, saying: 'Must we obey everything, as sheep obey the shears or a cow the milker's hands?'

She spoke upwards towards Hlangeni, but she was really talking to everybody gathered around, her voice drumming over them: 'Listen, it is said that the white man's laws and his weapons and his money make his heart bad, that for these things he has exchanged brotherhood, that with these things he can destroy manhood. But it is his own manhood, his own brotherhood which he has killed. So be it, but he has not killed ours. We are still a people. With laws and guns and money he knows nothing of people, does not sense the dignity of people. This inability to see mystifies him, baffles him, for he cannot understand it, and he is defeated because in him there is no heart, no dignity. He does not understand, he is afraid of it, so he laughs very loud at the dignity of the people; but it is a defeated laughter, a mask over the defeat in his heart. The evil one laughs to conceal his defeat even while he waves his gun and his authority over the people, and generally in the end, under cover of his unlaughing laughter, he retreats, unable to understand. And so against the evils of the bad one there is a defence and a remedy, the people's will and dignity, and it is possible for the heart to remain whole, the times to be good, the years to be fat.'

Watching from the rise where he stood with the shepherd, the man called Shilling Murile said, 'Hauw! I remember that one. That is Mma-Tau, the she-lion, as ferocious as ever.'

'A terrifying woman,' Madonele echoed. 'I keep out of her way at all times.'

The shepherd noticed that the other was rolling another cigarette out of the brown paper he took from his denims, the tobacco from the orange-coloured packet, and he coughed and shuffled watching the operation performed with so much skill. Having licked the cigarette into shape, the young man passed the tobacco to the shepherd, not looking at him, but watching what was going on below.

'Many times I received a slap from that she-lion's paw,' he said, lighting the handmade cigarette and blowing smoke. 'And there is no doubt that she will have her way here. Her roaring alone would frighten everybody into obedience.'

Madonele the shepherd was happily lighting his pipe, puffing ecstatically, and saying between puffs, 'Ai, that Mma-Tau, she went away from the village to the city and there was peace here. I do believe that the city could not abide her ferocity and was glad to see the back of her.'

Below them, past the stunted thorn trees and the side of Hlangeni's house, the woman was saying: 'They exist in a false happiness of guns and laws, they exist with false laughter, for the laughter is not really theirs. Do they know the meaning of their laws and their false happiness and their undignified laughter? The meaning is this: that men are of two kinds, the poor who toil and create the riches of the earth; and the rich who do not toil but devour it. The meaning is this: that the people demand their share of the fruits of the earth, and their rulers, of whom the white man is a lackey, a servant, refuse them a fair portion. And it is this: that the people insist, the rulers deprive them of work, drive them from their homes, and if they still resist, send their lackeys to shoot them down with guns.

'The meaning is this: that we know very well, who are awake, that life is both good and evil. Women, men, children, all who face their law and their weapons, their prisons and incarceration, feel the blood of rage in their veins, the rage of an invaded and despoiled people against the evil that has come among them. The rage in the blood, the blood is of the people, and law and guns have no blood.

'The evil is the law and the guns who ransack our homes, frighten our children, mistreat our women, humiliate the elders, arrest and jail the breadwinners and protectors. Must we obey the evil or must we obey the blood which is life?

'My brother Hlangeni says we must obey the law and the weapons, the evil. Can a people be obedient to evil? Bah, there is no dignity in that.'

Now there was a rustle among the villagers congregated in the encroaching dusk. Some of the old men rose to their feet and slapped dust from their clothes, peering at the vast woman as they leaned on gnarled sticks, while others pushed forward, commencing to chatter among themselves, gesticulating. All this Hlangeni watched, and he had a feeling of betrayal and defeat that crowded in on him, and he knew they would follow her and not him. Beside him even the councillor Kobe said: 'Hauw! The she-lion has roared.'

'It's not right, it is not proper,' Hlangeni said. 'A woman?'

But an old man was saying, 'Can we not live the past again? Tell us, can the past be recalled?'

'Listen,' Hlangeni cried from where he stood. 'The white Commissioner said that a train will await us at the station in town to take us to this new place. They will come here with their lorries to take us to the station.'

'Must we be taken like cattle?' somebody cried out.

Mma-Tau turned her great face up towards Hlangeni and the look in her eyes was not unkindly as she said, 'My brother, you and I are of one mother, and have been here all this time.' The great arms spread to embrace the village, the stunted trees, the sun-blistered cabins, the dust-laden hills beyond. 'You yourself have said, this is our land. Your own words asked, is it so terrible to love one's home? Were not our ancestors leaders before you? Are you not descended from warriors?'

'The times are different,' Hlangeni cried. '*They* rule us now.'

The woman nodded. 'Yes, the times are different. There is meaning in what you say, even though you do not know it. But I say this clearly, I shall not go from this land. That is what the times mean for me.'

'Who will stay with you, to defy them?'

'Listen, my brother, there are those who will follow my word, and there are those who will follow yours. It has come to that.'

'You have always been headstrong, defying all customs, traditions. I forbid any to follow you.'

'My brother, there are those among us who will follow the blood in their veins. Listen, you are chief here, and a chief should lead forward not back. If we go forward we may die, if we go back we may die; better go forward.'

'You do not respect me as a chief.'

'My brother, a chief is not a chief merely by custom and heredity, he is also a chief out of respect earned from his people. Come, show us that you are our leader, that you have the blood of the warriors of old time in your veins still.'

'Other folk obey the white man, why not you?'

'Listen, you have said it, the times are different. Soon all will come to see that, but you must be one of those to open their eyes.'

But Hlangeni called out over her head: 'Hear me, my people, it is foolishness to defy the white man. In a day we must go from here, even though this woman who is called my sister has been among you to talk against it. What can we do against the whites? Think on what I have said, it is better to obey.'

The crowd milled again, their voices mingling, the dust rising from under their feet in the evening light. The voice of the woman, Mma-Tau, rose above the rest.

'She will have her way,' Madonele the shepherd said, as they moved off in the receding light. The smoke was pleasant in his mouth and he felt happy.

'It is her thing,' the one called Shilling Murile replied, speaking morosely as he kicked up dust with his thick boots. 'I have a thing of my own.'

Ai, this is a strange one, the shepherd thought, but I am happy to be in his company. Pattering along in his ragged blanket and disreputable hat, his dry little toes digging into the warm earth, he realised that they were making for the old cemetery on the hill.

*

Now there was this bungalow of orange brick which, with its corrugated roof and twin front windows, gave the impression of a flushed face angry-eyed under an iron vizor. They lived in the middle-aged part of the city, a sort of no-man's-land between the concrete towers of adulthood and the flaking ruins of infancy. The jacarandas lining the streets did not relieve the atmosphere of embattlement which metal guards — ornate in places but still protective — gave the district. Bungalows where nervous ladies viewed the black houseboys and kitchenmaids as potential outriders to hordes of rampaging barbarians. Apprehension scuttled like mice behind the decorative curtains, and each creak of a floorboard, the crack of loose parquet, was a peal of alarm bells summoning the paranoia of perpetual siege. North, beyond the border the lily-livered Portuguese had given in to the howling mobs; fear began to nag like an itch in the groin of the continent.

But she was simply bored. Across the frontier of her boredom there was nothing. The sullenness of life made *her* itch. God, all these years in that place with the fancy ironwork over every aperture, like that whatchermacallit — chastity belt — she had read about in a story full of lute-playing minstrels and swooning ladies. Errol Flynn and Olivia De Havilland. She remembered those films years ago; but nowadays it was Clint Eastwood and Robert Redford, or the Ster De Luxe showing *Revenge Of The Mafia*.

She shared the native maid, Polly, with Mrs Muller next door. At least she could do her own ordering about when she was home.

Thank God the old bag was out of the way at last. Maisie sat under the striped awning of the open-air café and idly watched the movement beyond the stainless steel chairs, the plastic table-tops, while she thought of escape. Her mother had sold the shop when the Group Areas Law had made all the coloureds and Indians move from the district. It was to become an industrial zone. Of course the old woman had been clever enough to refuse to sell until the last minute when almost everybody had disappeared and the site was needed — even that shabby little corner — so she had got a good price. 'If those big shots want this plot they'll have to pay,' Mrs Barends scowled and clashed her dentures spitefully. The mean bitch had stuck to every penny of course, and now she was esconced in that tawdry hotel for old ladies — a bloody glorified old-age home — where she could pretend at retired gentility.

Well, she won't find me visiting her many Sundays, Maisie had promised herself. She sipped her milk-shake and thought, God, must I always be burdened with a lot of unglamorous pumpkins?

She felt the moisture in her armpits and the tiny trickles slithering down her rib-cage. Beyond the tables the sun lay like yellow dust on the footpaths, the street, the concrete and glass buildings quivering in the middle distance. The radio behind her was broadcasting the *Annie Get Your Gun* programme — advice to housewives on the use of firearms — and a voice was saying: ' . . . the Colt Woodsman is a point two-two calibre target pistol and perhaps a little too lengthy for carrying in a purse. . . .' That made her recall the time she had belonged to the gun club and there had been that bloody awful police instructor. He smelled of stale tobacco and there was the beginnings of a boil on his jawbone as he stood close to her, showing her how to point the pistol. He had been saying something about Smith and Wessons, and she could smell his breath, warm and sour. 'Don't jerk, squeeze slowly.' He had a gutteral Boer voice and she hated the sound of it and smell he gave off, which was probably why she had stopped going to the shooting lessons. Anyway she wasn't going around with a bloody great revolver like John Wayne, though she did eventually buy a little pistol, one you could stick in your bra or a stocking garter. 'One never knows when some terrible kaffir will run amok,' one of the women at the gun club said with contrived horror, looking comic wearing the big rubber ear-muffs. 'You'll probably enjoy it, you bitch,' Maisie thought. But she had bought the little Beretta all the same. James Bond, like James Bond. You can always join the army when things get to a dead-end, she thought now and broke the straw in her glass.

The voice on the radio said: 'Remember when aiming do not aim at the head but at the middle of the chest where the target is biggest. The jerk caused by the recoil. . . .' But she was not listening. Instead her eyes were on the man who had come up to one of the tables and was drawing out a chair. Dark hair long and fashionable, a vaguely familiar face, and she said. 'Donald. Donald Harris.'

The man turned and looked at her with slight puzzlement and then smiled, a toothpaste smile, and she was trying to identify him as always with some film star while he said, 'Why, it's Maisie, isn't it, hey? Little Maisie.'

He was coming towards her through the futuristic undergrowth of stainless steel and plastic where an Indian waiter lurked in ambush in the background. The man said, 'True as God, it's Maisie from the Plaza bio. But it isn't Donny Harris, I'm Wally Basson.'

'Wally Basson of course, yes. Glad you reckernised *me* at least.'

'Who wouldn't, man, who wouldn't?' The polished smile and a summery safari suit draping the bony frame: Wally Basson of course.

He was pulling up a chair, not bothering to ask permission; there was an air of flamboyancy about him, bravado — he could have been a buccaneer from some pirate film. The waiter was there with gloved hands holding the menu and drinks list like a subpoena, but Wally waved it aside — he could not be trapped. 'Not milk-shakes, for God's sake, baby. Bring us a couple of rum cocktails.'

'In this heat?'

'Heat, heat, who cares about heat? There's only one kind of heat I care about an' it don't come from the sun, hey.'

The toothpaste smile, the mock sinister look while she took a quick douse in the pool of her powder compact. He was a boy all right, she could tell. She remembered him again from those days. God, was that really her on the steps of the cinema with those boys? She said, coming up refreshed, 'I got you mixed up with Donald Harris. You ever see Donny Harris?'

'Oh, hell, *him*. Forget it. How are you getting on, Maisie, man? Hey, you look good, hey.' The eyes, clear and bright as a pair of new dice, were bold, insolent.

'I'm okay. Why, we all used to meet at the Plaza, you, me, Donny and all. What about Donny?'

A black woman with a baby slung in a shawl on her back sat

down in a box of shade across the street. Traffic sparkled in the sunlight as if studded with jewels. Maisie noticed a policeman, white helmet, breeches and boots, gun and sungoggles, patrolling the sidewalk, stop to tower over the black woman. Like something out of those space movies, Maisie thought absently. *Invaders From Mars*. The goggled monster prodded the black woman with a club, a grotesque extension of his hand. She struggled up, hoisting the infant, and went down the street among the short-sleeved, sunglassed pedestrians while the robot tramped on. The traffic crawled by, gleaming in the sun.

Wally Basson was saying as he offered her a cigarette: 'The bloody fool is in chooky.'

Maisie took the cigarette and looked at the flame of his gold lighter: 'What did you say? Who?'

'Donny Harris, hey. He's in bloody jail, true as God.'

'Jail? Him? But he was always such a nice and respectable boy.'

'Got himself mixed up with niggers. Coons. The damn fool though it was a good idea to help the darkies with trade unions or something, true as God. Reckoned they're having a rough time, hey. Politics. I only read it in the papers, I don't know the exact details. Illegal organisations and stuff. Communists. So he got ten years, I think — no, twelve.'

She said, momentarily aghast: 'Messing with blacks? But he's white, like us.' The memory of a black woman with a baby just seen flashed through her mind. 'Them?'

Wally shrugged, 'You never know with people. Anyway, it was in the papers.'

'Oh, I don't read things like that. The magazine part maybe, the comics on Sundays, Blondie and Dagwood. To think that nice Donny Harris could of gone and done a thing like that.'

The waiter came with the order and Donny Harris slid aside, an irksome memory. The rum cocktails made her a little tipsy and she felt the perspiration between her breasts. She giggled, the hard green eyes bright as tinsel. 'Garn, you trying to get me tight?'

That had been the start of it. Whenever Edgar was away there were the plush cinemas, the cocktail lounges, discothèques; over to the next province for the sea, *Cool Waters, The New Luxury Beachfront Hotel, Golden Sands;* across the border and gambling in Swaziland casinos — one couldn't go to Mozambique any more. There were parties in Wally's flat; lots of expensive plonk that inevitably led to other things. Things had moved quickly, but she didn't give a bladdy damn, hey. Bugger Edgar. God, to think how she had tried to get away from it all: the shop, her parents, the barricaded bungalow. She had made it, she thought, after trying all kinds of remedies for boredom. Even Devil's Church — witch's covens in old and derelict buildings with a former university student. 'Satan is for real, man. I got a lot of mates who are hooked on Satan.' But that had turned out a bore too afterwards. The ex-student had an unfurnished room with a worn mattress on the floor, scattered with shards of potato crisps. *Is there life after death?* the Sunday paper asked. Who cares?

Now Wally Basson said with his clinical smile (she recalled Edgar's samples: *Maclean Whiteness, It's the nicest colour for a smile*): 'Maisie, me and you we can go places, man. True as God.'

'Places where?' The green eyes turned on him. She had a suspicion that Wally's 'business' was not going so well any more.

'Up, baby, up. But what we need is a bit more capital, hey.'

'Oh! Are you broke then?'

'Broke? Dammit, no. But I lost a bit on that newfangled back-gammon dingus.'

'Well, you didn't know the game so well.'

'Well, it's a new thing. One got to get practice.'

'But outjie, what can *I* do? *I* can't help. All the money in our family is with my old woman.'

'Ja, I know, I know, *bokkie.*'

There was an awful feeling that he was thinking of dropping her. Perhaps she had become too expensive, so no more casinos, flash hotels where the jet-set circulated, the race-course, the drives in the shiny new Avenger. She thought desperately of the bungalow, the humdrum life, the suitcases of samples, Edgar proclaiming futilely that one had to 'get on'. 'Every man for himself.' Well, *he* hadn't got on, made it. And neither have you, Miss bloody Maisie. What the hell *you* doing? Getting favours from a gambling man with a smile? God, if Edgar dropped dead, the bugger, at least I'd have four thousand rands in insurance. Two thousand bloody pounds.

She asked, 'Things are going to be awright, isn't it?'

Wally said, 'Things? Sure, Maisie, sure. But we got to work together, hey.' He pinched her arm amorously.

'I know. You know I'm with you, Wally.'

'That's my girl, that's my girl. I got plans, true as God.'

'Plans?'

'Now look here. Me and you, we like the good life, isn't it? The shows, clubs, trips?'

'Naturally.'

'But it costs, hey. So we got to speculate to accumulate, there isn't no other way.'

'Oh, I reckon not.'

'There, you see? You got it. You got understanding, baby, true as God.' He smoothed out a fold in his newspaper. 'The way I see it, I mean the way I been looking at it is like this. There's a lot of guys with cash go to those places we go to. Right? Rich jokers. So maybe some of them want some extra fun.'

'Extra fun?'

'Like we can provide.'

'How d'you mean?'

'Look, there's you an' me. Now you a pretty good-looker, Maisie, and me, I got this flat. So maybe there's a bloke he wants a nice quiet evening in sort of private with a nice girl. So we got this flat and I could sort of go off somewhere....'

'Jesus Christ.' Her voice froze into gritty ice.

He said, 'Hell, honey, it's for both of us, isn't it? Man, they all respectable jokers. Businessmen, M.P.s maybe, rich jokers from others parts.'

'God almighty, you don't *mean* it.'

'Well, all right, no exactly, I reckon. It was just sort of an idea, true as God. Well, anyway, you — I mean we — can think about it, hey. I mean, there's no harm in thinking about it, you know.'

She walked from the bedroom, leaving him with the fillies and geldings. A headline below his onyx signet ring revealed: 'Strike Threatened'. In the carpeted living-room Tretchikoff's coolie girl smiled at her from the stippled wall over the sideboard which served as the drinks cabinet, the Oriental face slightly scornful across the sticky glasses on the coffee-table and the discarded stockings like reptilian moulting. Outside the glass door to the little balcony the sun was hard amber over the hazy skyline of the city. To the north spread the wealthiest suburbs: apartment blocks slung low and wide, islands of comfort surrounded by green lagoons of lawn, floodlights sequining the swimming-pools at night.

She leaned on the balcony wall eleven storeys up in the block of flats and felt the heat, tropic in intensity, like a branding-iron on her skin. The sky quaked and quivered. Or the roof of a lower building, children in shorts and swimsuits played in the harsh mid-morning sun, their heads gleaming like metal helmets, bronze, gold, dark steel, as they fired toy guns from the doorways of the deserted servant's quarters. Since the 'locations in the sky' had been abolished the roofs had become playgrounds for the young of the tenants.

A row of shouting youngsters dropped water bombs from the parapet to the pavement nine storeys below, trying to hear the paper bags burst. The imitated gunfire coughed from the line of doors.

If he died there'd be four thousand rands. Die? Edgar was fit as a horse. It struck her that she had seen in some film than an insurance company paid double if the insured died in some uncommon accident. Two times two thousand pounds, roughly speaking. *Here Jesus*, girl, you can set out on your own with that much; no useless, loudmouthed Edgar, no old bag of a stingy mother, and you wouldn't need Wally Basson to depend on for a flash life. With eight thousand rand, who needed Wally bloody Basson? Independence. You got to look after number one, that's what old Edgar always was on about, wasn't he? An accident. She felt hot and sweaty, but her thoughts kept her on the balcony. God, you're getting on; time you did something about it. Eleven floors below, the street moved. But she and Edgar lived in a bungalow. Lived: the jacarandas turning brown, the chattering women, children on the footpaths, kaffir maids in the back gardens licking condensed milk from slices of Hovis. Below her the children fired their toy guns. Did they pay double for a gunshot accident? But she had to look at the dingus first, the policy; read it carefully.

She did have the little pistol from the gun club. Maybe she could pretend she couldn't handle it properly and Edgar could show her and it could go off, accidental like. Something like that. No, no. What the *hell* are you thinking? In spite of the heat, she shuddered with fright and tore herself from the balcony as if caught in a sudden deluge of iciness.

She went to dress in the bathroom. From the bedroom Wally, sticky and naked, called out over *Runners and Betting:* 'What's the hurry, poppie? Your old man isn't due home till tomorrow, hey.'

Her laugh was a little cracked, her throat throbbing like a frog's. 'We should go to church, man. There's a day of prayer, remember.'

'Day of bladdy prayer, my foot, There's better things to do.'

'I was only joking, man.'

She looked at herself, working the facial muscles as she only did when she looked in a mirror. You're getting on. She looked washed-out without make-up, like a tea cloth. Her jaw was beginning to fold. She traced the jawbone with a fingertip, searching out the tiny dent halfway along its line. That is where is starts to go: that hollow becomes a gap and suddenly the chin and the jaw separates and you have the face of an old woman. Old. Age crept up behind her like a werewolf; Dracula lurked in the sunset of approaching years. Tears of self-pity prickled in her eyes.

'Turn on the radio, baby,' Wally called from the bedroom. Orders, she thought, now he's giving damn orders. You might as well join the ... army. They took women and made all the decisions for you, too.

Springbok Radio ended something by O'Sullivan and replaced him with an advertising jingle: 'Kelly's tyres are tough. Kay, ee, double-el, why.' That's what you got to be, *meisie*, to beat them: tough.

*

The back street was in darkness. An electric lamp at each end and nothing in between left a sweltering stretch of heavy black. There were few lights on in the windows of the old-fashioned houses which took up one side, and these did not extend into the gravel street. From the back gardens opposite the houses the chorus of cricket sounds clattered in the hot night. Glow-worms trembled against the dark. *Agterstraat* had been the original street of the little town before the railway had come, the hotel, the shops with their plastic blinds and gaudy displays, the cottages of railway workers, the Bantu Commissioner, the post office, the police station, the garage. Other houses were scattered among the trees but what was now referred to as the Back Street had been the main thoroughfare of the old settlement.

Walking in the cloying darkness, Hannes Meulen thought that something should be done about getting more lights into the street. He would have to raise it with the management Board. His empty pipe clamped between strong teeth he strolled towards the Steen house. He knew exactly where to go in the darkness, his rubber-soled golf-shoes crunching the gravel quietly, but a few more street lights would brighten up things. The older folk would be able to stroll out on nights like these. These thoughts were merely asides, for he was really looking forward to seeing Rina again. Even a few days away in the city had caused him pain of longing, and he yearned for the day when they would finally be married. They had already planned to marry before the elections: a Member of Parliament should have a wife.

They had known each other since childhood, had grown up together, separated only when they had gone their separate ways for further education, meeting again and drawing naturally together, so that everybody accepted their mating as a foregone conclusion. Together they had attended rugby matches, danced in the local *volkspele*, the folk-dance club. He recalled sentimentally those years ago as a boy in khaki shorts, hair tousled, when he had watched her climb a tree like a tomboy, a bronze-coloured plait come adrift, giggling down at him with blue eyes and freckles.

He was a farmer's son and she the daughter of *Oom* Kasper Steen, who had retired early in life, having come by a tidy sum in the form of a legacy. Then Oom Steen had been in sheep too, but he had never had very much enthusiasm for it and had sold out as soon as he had come into that inheritance, settling down in the old townhouse with his daughter. Hannes Meulen lived on with his father and younger sister on the family sheep farm. He knew sheep, but his father also had other interests in life and he had learned to emulate him.

Beside sheep, Christofel Meulen had been interested in people, and especially after his wife had died bearing his daughter, had become engaged in public affairs. Public affairs related to the growing town, the new people moving in, railway workers, the church, the new Coloured location, the 'kaffirs' still inhabiting the nearby lands. Public affairs involved the news from the cities, the capital, the struggle of the *volk* to gain ascendancy in Parliament. These things were something apart from sheep-dip, the shearing, the transport of bales of wool, although they did affect prices at the sales, the cost of railway transport, the world market.

The boy Hannes learned sheep-farming and listened to what his father spoke about to the locals, tried to fathom the activities of this large man with the rough, red face like beef and salt-and-pepper hair. The father loved the land: to him country was not only a geographical entity, an anthem, celebrations of Dingane's Day, the day of Blood River. For him country was a matter of who owned the flat, dreary red and yellow plains and the low, undulating hills, the grass and the water. This was a heritage which had been gained through the sacred blood of their ancestors and the prophetic work of God. It had come to their fathers through the musket and the Bible; they had come into this land like the followers of Joshua. Any other conception was anathema.

To church every Sunday, Hannes in his black *kisklere*, looking out for Rina. She would be there in her Sunday dress with the low waist and the bow, her mother in black. His own father wore his best suit with butterfly collar and funereal bow tie. After the service the men talked outside under the trees in the square, near the Boer War monument, while the children flitted about like birds.

He remembered the meetings held in the schoolhouse on Saturdays. Only the menfolk went to these meetings; such matters were not the affair of women. There were farmers and other men, all in riding-breeches and grey shirts, like a uniform. His father wore the breeches and grey shirt too and spoke at these meetings. The men opposed a war against Germany. The Germans stood for unity of the race, of the chosen people of God. Any war against Germany would uphold ideas of miscegenation, of bastardisation, of liberal thoughts entertained by the British and the Jews. Thus the ideas of Hitler coincided with those of the men at these meetings. 'The Afrikander volk is not the work of man, but the work of God,' his father shouted, his red face writhing with passion. 'We shall prevail.' All the men at the meetings shouted and raised their right arms and hands.

When the boy was fifteen his father had been killed. His horse, frightened by something, had reared and thrown him. Farm-hands searching for him when he had not returned home for the noon meal found him sprawled in the red karoo dust, his neck broken. From all over the district people had gathered at the funeral. His associates wore their breeches and grey shirts defiantly and gave the stiff-armed salute over the grave. After that the farm had resorted back to the care of the grandfather, but the old man seemed disinterested, given to daydreaming about bygone times rather than considerations for the welfare of the land he had settled. Gradually he had withdrawn into a sort of private world of his own, a world which existed only in his disintegrating mind, a perpetual dream.

I am near forty, Hannes Meulen thought, it is my turn now. The farm was a going concern, except of course for the present drought, but there had been droughts before; his sister had been married off years ago and was happily settled; he himself had made strides. He had joined the national party after graduation, the nearest thing to what his father had upheld, and he was a prospective Member of Parliament for this constituency. Marriage to the girl he cared for and a public future lay ahead of him.

The Steen house had a high stoep reached by stone steps at one end, a white gabled front with multi-paned windows in the façade decorated with plaster moulding and pilasters. The thatched roof was solid and old Steen had it regularly inspected. Lights burned behind the curtains of the casement windows and a radio played broadcast music. When he used the brass knocker he heard footsteps and waited, his heart commencing to quicken inside him. She would not send the servant to open the door, since he was expected, and Kasper Steen would be in his easy-chair or by the radio, so when the door opened there was Rina.

His heart turned inside him and she was saying a little breathlessly, '*Liefling, liefling.*'

He held her arms and kissed her upturned mouth gently, then a cheek, and she said: 'A naughty boy, you should have come from the station.' She was drawing him into the hallway calling back into the house, 'Papa, it's Hannes, he's come.'

'I thought that I'd go to the hotel and wash up, get the train dust out of my skin,' he said.

'Isn't this heat frightful? Well, come then, you must tell us everything that's happened.'

He took her arm, his eyes admiring her. Firm young breasts, not an ounce of fat on her body and the past boyishness of her limbs had softened into beautiful lines of a well-made woman. Her curly bronze hair gleamed in the lamplight, and her nose was peeling a little from sunburn, but there was a certain demureness about her mouth, an innocence which one expected to find in a well brought up Boer woman.

She would make a good wife, he thought happily. He loved her and she would bear his children. They would live at the farm and go travelling about the country, of course, when his public duties allowed him to take her with him. Otherwise she would oversee the farm, potter about in the kitchen garden and grow flowers — she loved flowers — or experiment with new recipes, make rusks, *biltong* and preserves, or turn the house upside down with spring-cleaning.

Laughing happily, she led him to the interior of the house. She smelled clean and fresh in spite of the hot night. '*Papa is in die*

59

sitkamer.' The lounge was off the hallway, full of armchairs, pouffes, a big carved sideboard of a past century, a big gilt mirror over the cold fireplace, and a chandelier hanging from the ceiling which was high and on beams.

Kasper Steen rose from the armchair where he had been reading when his daughter came in with Hannes Meulen. He was a short, wide man with thin grey hair swept back on his long head, and he had heavy jowls and a big nose, and with his pouched, moist eyes, he had the look of an old *aardwolf*. In spite of the heat he wore formal clothes, a neat grey suit, his shirt-collar shiny and starched, his cuffs carefully displayed. It was as if, having given up farm life, he now wished to demonstrate permanently that he was no *duinemol*, no bumpkin; that he was no mere clodhopper smelling of sheep-dip and cattle dung. He read the Afrikaans newspapers regularly, and books from his daughter's school stock. He smiled at Meulen with his neat dentures, thinly, as if heartiness might spoil the impression he wished to convey.

'There you are, Hannes,' he said. 'How goes it?'

'Oom Kasper,' the handsome man returned, taking the hand of his prospective father-in-law in a formal shake. He should already have been calling this man 'Dad' as other young men did, already accepted into the household, but he had never been able to bring himself around to doing that. The customary 'Uncle' for elder men was the nearest he could get. He thought that he would have to urge on the wedding arrangements in order to take Rina away to his farm, so that he would not have to face up to this formal man whenever he wished to see her.

'Rina,' Steen said to the young woman. 'Bring us the peach brandy.'

'On such a hot night, and before dinner? It's hot enough to make the crows yawn.'

'Ach, it's nothing, and your young man can do with a little something.' He smiled again at Meulen while Rina busied herself at the sideboard. 'I suppose things went well?'

'As far as I can assess,' Meulen answered. 'Affairs ought to go in our favour. What does Oom read?'

Steen looked at the book still held in his hand. 'Oh, just a novel. It's from Rina's schooldays — a story by Potgieter.' He motioned towards the armchairs. 'But sit, man. You know you are at home.'

He went back to the chair in which he had been reading and Meulen took another near him, crossing his legs comfortably.

'May I smoke?' He always asked the older man's permission, another thing which irked him secretly. He smiled up at Rina when she came with the little glasses of liqueur. She left the bottle on the miniature table nearby.

'Dinner will be ready in a minute. I'll call you when I'm ready.'

Watching with longing as she went from the room tossing the bronze curls, bare legs flashing with her light gait, then Meulen turned back to Steen, saying, *'Gesondheid'* before taking a sip from the little glass. He put it down again and filled his pipe from a leather pouch and said, 'Well, the corporation has accepted the geologist's report. They accept that the land in question must hold certain mineral deposits.'

'Goed, goed,' Steen nodded. 'That is one blessing.'

Meulen held a lighter to his pipe and puffed. 'They will set up the company, fifty-two per cent held by the government through them and the other forty-eight will be offered to the public. I, of course, pointed out that you and I are interested in buying a substantial amount of those shares.'

'Allemagtig, you did well, boy.'

'As soon as the kaffirs are moved — '

'We call them Bantu now, boy,' Steen said and smiled again. 'Things have changed.'

Meulen smiled. 'As soon as the Bantu have been moved, the development of that area will commence. As you know, by request of the people here I myself went to the magistrate to ask that they be moved. He in turn referred it to the Chief Commissioner who required a list of names. The magistrate supplied the names, all of them, and then the matter went to the Department of Community Affairs. The surveyor's report helped, naturally.' He discovered that he was speaking in an offical manner, relating what had happened in a precise way, and thought that it was a necessary characteristic of a Member of the *Volksraad*.

'Those black things will move, of course,' Steen remarked.

'Naturally. The Department made arrangements with the railways for a train to take them from here. The local farmers will supply lorries to bring them to the station and they ought to go tomorrow.'

'Altogether splendid,' Steen said, and poured more of the peach brandy. 'This will help you to become more popular with the local folk, even though the opposition is not putting up a candidate here.'

'Well, we have all been in these parts for generations, and everybody knows us now.'

'Ja. Tell me, how is your grandfather? I haven't heard of the Oupa for a little time now.' Now with the brandy inside them they felt relaxed.

'Oh, he's hanging on. He doesn't want to leave the old house, and I don't want to disturb him. Rina and I will live in the *Niewehuis*, but I think she will have to look in on the old man as well, It won't be a burden, he prefers to be left alone.'

'Aai, he really is old.'

Rina came in smiling, 'Come on then, food is on the table.' The men rose and Meulen knocked out his pipe. Steen's face was a little flushed. She took Meulen's arm and they followed her father into the dining-room.

Under the lights and the ceiling beams the solid stinkwood furniture shone with polish, the cutlery gleamed on the table, two originals of the veld in bloom hung in gilt and plaster frames on the spotlit walls. At the end of the room french-windows, left open to let in the night air and the sounds of insects through the screendoor, looked out from between heavy, parted curtains towards the dark back garden, the moonlight bright on wilting grenadilla vines.

The men sat down, one at each end of the table, and Rina sat between them. A coloured servant woman brought in the soup and Steen said, 'Let us give thanks to almighty God.' They bowed their heads over the plates and he muttered the grace, then poured wine for Meulen and himself. 'It's not a bad white, not too dry. They make a good wine in the Western Cape, just as good as the imported stuff.'

'Hannes,' Rina said as they ate, 'You must help me.'

'You know I will, *my skat*.'

'The Department of Nature Conservation wrote and they want me to take charge of the plan to rescue plants and flowers from the drought.'

'That's a big job,' Meulen said, smiling at her. 'But I'm sure you'll handle it. Go on.'

'Well, there are hundreds and hundreds of wild flowers out in the veld and they'll die from thirst if they're not moved to places where they can be preserved. There are aloes, cycads, even orchids, which must be transplanted. The idea is to mount an expedition to go out into the veld, find the plants and flowers and move them to certain public gardens and parks for preservation.'

'Altogether a good idea. I've read about it. So you're overseeing things here?'

'Well, with some help. I shall go around talking to people forming a body. Naturally you men will have to do the hard work, digging, and lifting the big ones. Bread trees are enormous.'

'Naturally the men will have to do the hard work,' her father chuckled. 'Your young man has muscle.'

'The thing is,' Rina said, dabbing her mouth, 'We need lorries, Land Rovers, you know? You must donate us a couple of lorries, Hannes. Will you?'

'Trucks I can lend you,' Meulen said while the rest of the meal was brought in. 'When you're ready. But at the moment some of the trucks have taken sheep over to where there is more water, and I have promised two lorries to the Commissioner to transport the kaffirs tomorrow.'

'Oh, there will be time, but I must know beforehand, you understand? Well, I shall put Meneer Hannes Meulen down for lorries. That should move the rest of the folk to helping out.'

'There,' her father said. 'You see you are going to have a wife who will out do you in public activities, so be careful, son.'

Meulen chuckled, 'She can help me with my speeches.'

'What — about wild flowers?' Rina asked and they laughed.

The rest of the meal was *frikadells*, yellow rice cooked with raisins, boiled vegetables, beet salad and apricot chutney. They passed dishes among them and Steen called on the servant to bring the peach brandy from the lounge. He said, helping himself to salad 'Ja, you will go into the Volksraad at an important time of our history. The world is changing and it expects us to change with it.'

'It all depends what they mean by change. We should be willing to see things in a new light, but nothing should be done at the expense of our *kultuur*, our honour. In the cities the blacks are stirring, they complain about money, wages, and rights. We are doing our best to give them rights.'

Rina said, 'When I was at college there were a few boys who proposed the strangest things. That three million of us white people could never go on controlling the Bantu. That we would have to give in to them and make the best of it.'

'There is a tendency to this imported liberalism, even in our Afrikaans universities nowadays,' Steen said and sipped some brandy. 'Perhaps it is a sign of the times, I don't know. But what can be done with a people who a century ago had not discovered the wheel? Countries overrun by barbarism sink to barbarism, that is the experience of history. Look what happened on this continent, in the north, when the Europeans withdrew. Now it is coming nearer, the Portuguese are in for it. Will our turn come next? As you say, the Bantu are on the move in spite of what we are doing for them. What we are going to need is strength, determination, to preserve our people, our civilisation.' He drew a new handkerchief from his breast pocket and wiped his perspiring forehead. The glow-worms flickered beyond the screen door.

'It is a pity that our friends overseas, whom we have allowed to benefit from what we have done here, do not see that we cannot adopt the same outlook they do towards their own problems,' Hannes Meulen said. 'They want their cake and eat it, as the Englishman says.' He speared a rissole on his fork and looked down the table. 'Can we believe in ourselves if we also allow ourselves to be influenced by the changing way of life in their countries? Our course is set. What might appear to be divergencies, faltering, like Rina's schoolmates, are entirely superficial, I'm sure. After all, the foundation and the cement of our people, which is as everlasting as the monument we set up in the capital in honour of our forefathers, that cement and foundation is the ethic of our racial, cultural and religious purity.'

'The problem facing us today, it seems,' Steen said, pushing aside his plate, 'is that we are being beset by one of the most difficult of our time. I mean this striving after so-called liberation from all bonds that discipline people. This liberalistic spirit has taken possession of many people in many countries and is showing signs here.'

Hannes Meulen smiled at Steen over the dishes, the napery, the leftovers of rissoles and beet salad. He was thinking of his father; of the men in grey shirts around the grave in the cemetery by the church, the rest of the mourners looking at them a little curiously; the boy with sober face refusing to shed tears in the presence of the elders. He saw the beef-red face writhing with pounding blood at the school meetings, and said smiling at Rina, 'The Afrikaner people is not the work of man, it is the work of God. We shall prevail.'

'Amen to that,' Steen said, while the servant brought in the fruit salad and cream.

Rina had listened in silence to the last interchanges between the two men. Except for her remark about these boys at college, she added nothing else, knowing that these things were really the affairs of the men. She was wearing Hannes' engagement ring and that meant that she would stand by him, in everything he wished to do. That was her duty. Her college education would be an asset to him too. She would be his good wife and the mother of his children, live under his protecting arm, and she would watch him grow to something in this community, and her heart fluttered with pride.

'Well,' Steen said after the pudding, pushing back his chair. 'I'm going to my room to read, leaving you two lovebirds alone.'

'Aren't you going to have a little cup of coffee?' Rina asked.

'Tell the *meid* to bring it to my room.'

'I will naturally see Oom at the service tomorrow,' Meulen said.

'But you can fetch us and we'll all go together,' Rina said.

'That's a good idea. Well, have another brandy, Hannes, and good night, son.'

'Sleep restfully, Oom.'

Rina got up and kissed her father dutifully on a cheek and saw him to the door. She gave the servant instructions about coffee and came back to where Meulen stood at the table with a glass of liqueur. He raised it at her, smiling. 'To you, my treasure.' He put his free arm about her waist and felt its slenderness, the fragility of her ribs, and the beat of her heart. Her face blushed shyly as his fingertips brushed the side of a breast.

'*My skat*,' she said up at him, her hair bright bronze in the light. 'My treasure, too.'

*

On the brown hillside the cemetery rambled among the spiny thorns, scattered milkstones, the dry undergrowth that curled like charred paper in the heat. It was a cemetery because there were shallow mounds of dry earth and warped and broken headboards, broken crosses, heaped stones and empty jam jars, cracked vases, tin cans. There were newer graves, quickly identifiable because the turned soil had a comparative newness about it, the wild flowers had not quite wilted, the wooden tablets still held laboriously-painted names of the dead. Now the heaped stones and weathered boards threw shadows among the crumbling graves and the rusting crockery of death, as the dusk unfolded its purple shroud.

The shepherd Madonele crouched in the dust by a karoo bush and sucked placidly at the long pipe, savouring the taste of tobacco from its tall bowl. His skinny fingers scratched contentedly now and then under the ragged blanket, while the little eyes gazed ahead contemplatively from under the old hat. Around him the cicada insects were starting to chirrup but he did not notice these sounds, being used to them, and he did not look in the direction of Shilling Murile, thinking, at such a time a man wishes to be alone with what belongs to him.

Shilling Murile sat apart on a small boulder. He had unlaced his boots and pulled them off and he stretched his legs, wiggling his sweaty toes. From here he could see the whole countryside: the faraway smudge of mountains in the gathering dusk with the first stars blinking palely above them; the low yellow-brown hills mottled with shadows that spilled up their slopes from folds and crevices, the trees where the town lay alongside the railway station, the water pump, the church steeple; the huddled building of the Meulen farm. Over all the first gloom of night rolled cautiously forward after the long hot day.

I will do this some thing, he thought and rolled the bitterness in his mouth as if it was something to relish. Hatred sat behind the bleak eyes and watched through the obscuring brown panes; hatred was a friend to be given shelter, nurtured and petted as the old-time diviners petted the avenging rhingals; hatred crouched like a patient leopard, waiting, but alive with the coursing blood of bitter memory. He was at one with the graves, the battered headboards with doom peeling off them: Death lay at his feet and waited to be aroused.

Once love had been laid away in one of the graves, but now love had mouldered, decomposed and fallen away to leave only the bare teeth of grinning revenge; what had been a brother was now a collection of knuckles and ribs, shin and femur, and pelvis without manhood, without a name except the remnants of paint on a rotten and crumbling plank.

A red drop of sun lingered on the horizon, then spread, seeped over and was gone, and the sky was ablaze over the place where it had sunk and the dark crept over the sky from the eastern horizon to stain the land. The hills dropped slowly away to the karoo bushes, the camel-thorn, the detritus of sandstone and basalt, so that the land took on a look of smoothness under the soft cloth of the night.

We walked this way many times, Shilling Murile thought. They had grown up together and had herded the village sheep along the scrubby hillsides, had taken the puberty rites together and had suffered stoically away from the village. They had herded sheep for the white farmers and had built fences, sensing little of the stubborn encroachment taking place. They had brewed beer and had got merrily drunk sometimes, tittering behind their hands as the mother had scolded. They had gone hunting with the white men, carrying their guns, shouldering the game.

He could not carry much, Shilling Murile thought, and he had always been a little weak in the chest. During the cold season he would cough and his nose ran, and he had to be wrapped up and wear shoes. No, Timi had not been a hard case, but they were always together.

When Oupa Meulen's granddaughter married and extra kaffirs were needed to help with the menial chores of the celebration, Shilling Murile had taken his brother Timi along. There were sheep to be slaughtered, cases of liquor to be collected from the railway station, windows to be cleaned, the big marquee tent to be raised, a host of duties which the blacks carried out all day on the eve of the wedding and through the night, until the day saw everything in readiness for the festivities.

The centre of the celebrations was the Niewehuis which the old man's son had had built as times had changed, prosperity increased, but Oupa Meulen never bothered to set a foot in it. Old and withered, he now sat on the near-ruined stoep of the original farmhouse which he had set up himself when he had first come into this part of the country, and watched from the old armchair wrapped in a shawl, his half-blind, rheumy eyes trying to take in what was happening. He had no truck with the new ways and only tolerated the decisions and actions of his son Jacob. He had outlived his son, that was proof enough of the falsity and baselessness of modern ways; he had fought the blacks and the British and refused to become reconciled to their presence in the country, and he bore only the attentions of the old Nama retainer, Koos, who was as old and withered as he was and who lived in the back of the crumbling farmhouse. Dried out and stringy, Oupa Meulen was as bloodless and tough as biltong, the jerked meat he had lived on for most of his early years, and seemed almost stubbornly to refuse to leave this earth.

As for his grandchildren, Hannes and Berta, they were not a new generation, descendants, an extension of himself, they were merely accidents of nature, accepted strangers, they did not belong with the brittle memories of faraway years which he kept flickeringly alive in the bony, dry and mummified confines of his shrunken skull. He had heard from Koos that the *jongnoi*, the young mistress, was going to live in the city after her marriage, but that was to be expected, although he presumed the girl would want his blessing too. But what brought him out onto the stoep, aided by the equally shrunken monkey of a Nama, was the curiosity to hear the goings-on of a wedding, for it stirred up certain ashes in his feeble mind, exposed the distant event of his own like embers found under the remains of an old fire.

Early in the morning the wedding guests started arriving, most of them having come a long way, many from as far as the city. They came in cars, lorries, pick-up trucks; there were automobiles from the city, and estate-wagons their shininess dulled by red dust; but the old man sitting apart in front of the old house saw them as blurred figures through his fading eyes, heard the called greetings, the laughter, the growing hubbub. The aroma of roasting meat rose from the grills over the open fires. They would drink Cape wine and brandy, beer, imported whisky and champagne.

From the wide entrance-way of the feed-barn the blacks who were not appointed as servants, who had done all the heavy work, also watched the gaiety from a distance, while they became merry on bottles of filched liquor.

'It is not — it is not a proper wedding,' a man hiccuped, wiping his mouth on a ragged sleeve. 'There is no dancing. Where is the dancing? There should be dancing.'

'That will come later,' the lad Timi told him. 'The *nkosizana* has asked an orchestra to come from the city.'

'Why is the young lord giving the orders? Surely it should be the grandfather who still owns this place? Look at him there, yonder, perched like a crow overseeing things. It's not a proper wedding, there is no dancing.'

They had drunk several bottles of Cape sherry out of sight inside the barn and several of them were trying to perform a traditional bridal dance, kicking up dust and scattering lucerne.

The one who was speaking belched and said again, 'Neither have seen any *ilobolo*. Where is the bride-price? There is no dancing and no cattle. These *amalungu* do nothing properly.'

'There is too much dust,' the one called Shilling Murile called out to those dancing inside the barn. 'Besides, it is not you who are getting married today.'

Timi giggled and drank from the neck of a bottle, passed it on and said happily: 'No ilobolo, how fortunate. That Ndala had to go all the way to the city to work in order to raise money for the bride-price.'

The one who had spoken about dancing said, 'In the city our women also get married wearing the white dresses as these do.'

'It is the modern times,' Shilling Murile laughed and took the bottle. He was feeling happy too and he drank deep.

'Modern times,' the other man said tipsily. 'Modern times, without dancing. There should be dancing.'

'I told you it will come,' Timi said. 'They will dance in the big tent where they've laid a floor, did we not work at laying down that floor?'

'It is not like the old times,' the man said, belching again. 'White dresses.'

The old times, the old man thought painfully. The guests started arriving soon after sunrise. The carts, wagons drew up on the *werf*, the line of saddles of horsemen started along the wall of the farmhouse. As noon draws near the line of saddles has extended and the ox-waggons and Cape-carts stand under the trees. There are few people for there are not many families in the sparsely settled parts, but everybody is shaking hands and being given coffee, the elder women, big and heavy as percherons, are perspiring under their bonnets, the younger chattering, exchanging gossip. There is a flock of children fluttering about like doves, over-seen by servants. Everybody becomes more and more excited as they wait for him to arrive with the bride. From the open fires comes the smell of cooking, mugs of coffee move from hand to hand all the time, and then at last here he is with his new wife, sitting proud and smiling in the horse-drawn wagon, rolling into the yard from the distant church amid the whoops, cheers, and the firing of guns. The smell of powder and roast hangs in the air with that of dust kicked up by the guests.

The old man hears the cheers as his granddaughter arrives with her husband of a few hours, but he does not see the machines, the billowing dress and bridal veil, the pastel shades of the brides-maids, the smart city suits of the men; he sees these only as ghostly blurs and the true picture is that of himself and his own bride stepping solemnly up onto the stoep, into the house and the marriage chamber with the decked-out bed and the chairs where they sit while each guest, clad in old-fashioned Sunday clothes preserved in wooden *kists* for such occasions, is individually introduced to them, to wish them happiness, to kiss the bride and groom.

The feast — lamb, pumpkin, string-beans, home-brewed brandy, preserves, begins around the table in the *voorkamer*, the front room; and when it is over, everything is taken out, the dung floor cleared for the dancing. There is a fiddle and a concertina — who were the two who had played? — and the dancing goes on in the light of tallow candles, the young couples whirling and skipping while bearded old men and bonneted women look on from the sidelines, feet tapping. The surface of the dung floor has been churned up and they cough in the fine dust.

At midnight the bride was led to the marriage chamber by her senior female relations, prepared for bed, and the lights are blown out. Now he is brought, clamped in his tight suit, string-tie, to the chamber door by the best man who has a lately-grown beard and whiskers and looks deliberately solemn. Karel, the old man remembers now, Karel who had died at Spioonkop years later. He bolts the door behind him and stands in the darkness, listening to the merriment outside which will go on for the rest of the night. The barbecue lunch is over, the toasts have been drunk, and the bar set up in the marquee tent is out of sight behind the crowd of guests. The hired orchestra has arrived at last, *Hendrik Smit en sy orkes*, and the afternoon resounds with the music, shouts, laughter, whoops. Here is no fiddle and concertina, but trumpet, saxophone, piano-accordian, bass and drums, and their rhythm sends the birds flapping. Besides the old-time *vastrap* and *tickeydraai*, there is the rock-and-roll and the cha-cha-cha. The milling guests perspire, empty beer-cans and discarded bottles begin to appear in the big yard. A *jukskei* contest has started under the trees, yoke-pegs tossed at a target which is a stake on the ground.

Sometime in the afternoon an apparition appears to the old man crouched in the shade by his front door on the stoep of the old house. There is a girl in flowing white as if she is wrapped in a rustling cloud, but he does not see the flushed happiness in her face, and the young man with her is a figure out of focus so that he does not recognise the look of smiling embarrassment, the stiff, formal bow as the girl draws him forward. The old man hears voices, breathless and excited. He does not know these guests; they must have moved lately into these parts. Where is Karel? Karel should be introducing them. It was kind of them to come, he hoped that they would be attended to.

'Oupa, Oupa,' the girl is saying softly, in a voice which is a mixture of love and sadness.

She takes one of his hands — it is like a dried-out chicken-claw and he croaks, '*My kind*, my child,' half-recognising her now.

The shadows move across the werf and there is a cheer as the bride and groom, red with laughter, climb into their car to drive away for the honeymoon. Now the merriment goes on with renewed enthusiasm, all restraints dropped.

Inside the feed-barn most of the men had fallen into an intoxicated sleep, sprawled against the walls and stretched out in the scattered hay, among the bales of lucerne grass, limp and ragged, like fallen scarecrows. One of the black serving-women had sneaked out two bottles of brandy from the wedding celebration and they had finished those, and now they belched and snored and grumbled in their sleep. Below the barn and across the big farmyard the sounds of festivity came from the marquee tent, the clack and thump of the jukskei game under the trees, the shrieks of children dodging among the buildings and the parked traffic.

'Let us go,' Shilling Murile said swaying while he nudged his brother Timi awake with his foot.

Gulping, blowing spittle, and sitting up, saying, 'Where? Where?'

'Back to the village, or just sleep somewhere,' the other said. 'One needs air after this drinking, besides I am tired of listening to that music.'

'My head goes round and round,' Timi said and sat with his face hanging between his knees. 'I would rather sleep here. And see, you have a bottle in your pocket.'

'Some wine left over. Come on, boy, let us go. My head aches too, so let us go and find some water. Besides, when the *nkosi* Meulen discovers that we have been stealing his wine and brandy there will be trouble. These other fools will suffer for it.'

'Hauw, what a terrible thing this liquor does to one. It is really the *tokoloshe*, eh? My head goes round as if spirits are chasing each other within it.'

'Come on, we will sleep somewhere else, out in the hills.'

'*Yebo*, but hold on to me, my brother.'

Swaying against each other and dragging themselves out through the rear of the barn, they stumbled barefoot up a slope in their ragged clothes while the sounds of the wedding celebration dropped away behind them. A short stumbling walk and they had to sit down in the shade for a while, mumbling and retching into the dust while the shadows swarmed in the hills. They drank from the bottle. It was an adventure and, being inexperienced, so much liquor made them feel more ill than merry, yet it produced a feeling of boldness. Then they dragged themselves to their feet and moved on, while Timi broke into a mumbling ditty: '*O, you woman who dwells over there, what do you beat that makes such noise?*' And his brother answered, singing, drunkenly, '*It is my dress I beat....*'

'See,' Timi said, 'what have we here?'

'They are sheep,' Shilling Murile told him.

They hung on the pole-gate and watched the sheep shuffling placidly in the barbed-wire kraal. Beyond the growth of thorny aloes and bread trees the music and laughter of the wedding still beat against the gathering evening. The sheep moved, circling each other, rotating in the pen, sensing the presence of the men, and Timi was singing, watching the sheep, '*What dress is that, that makes such a noise? The poor sheep,*' he giggled, 'They did not come to the wedding, they did not dance.'

'*Aibo,*' said his brother, 'No, they did not, what a shame.'

'They should dance,' Timi said drunkenly. 'Everybody should be dancing. Let the sheep dance.' He wagged a finger at his brother. 'All should dance.'

'Truly, everybody should dance,' Shilling Murile laughed and he was dragging the gate open and stumbling in among the sheep, waving the bottle and calling out, 'Dance, dance, my sheep, everybody dance.'

The sheep milled, crowded the pen, bleating and struggling against each other, and Timi was stumbling among them too, yelling, 'Dance, sheep, dance.' The two young men lurched around the kraal, laughing and waving, and the sheep crowding each other broke through the gate and bundled out into the open with the two prancing among them, driving them on, shouting, '*Eyapi! Eyapi!*' Dust rose over the kraal setting them coughing and laughing while the herd scampered away, scattered by intervening trees and clumps of cacti, and the brothers went off in the other direction, giggling and swaying, slapping each other's backs, singing snatches of song.

With the sun gone down the air was sharp and biting and they shivered in their tattered shirts sitting in the dust by the side of the farm road, backs against fence-posts. Somewhere in the distance there was still the faint sound of the wedding orchestra, the sky was light purple and there were no stars yet; a breeze stirred the stiff grass, sent clumps of thorn rolling across the darkening fields.

The younger one, Timi, sneezed and blew his nose into the dust and sneezed again, while Shilling Murile said happily, 'Take some more of the bottle, it will warm you up. It is good medicine here.' He drank some himself, tipping the bottle up.

'No more,' Timi said and shook his head limply. 'It makes my brain go round and round.' He shook his head again and it lolled about as if his neck had turned to loose rope. His nose was running and he wanted to curl up somewhere where it was warm and sleep for a long time. He drew up his knees, wrapped his arms about his legs and shivered.

'I will finish it then,' Shilling Murile said and hiccuped before he emptied the bottle.

Down the road the dust boiled up behind a motor vehicle and headlamps grew brighter as it drew near, and they heard the sound of the motor and the clash of gears as it rumbled towards them. The glare of the headlights made them squint and they coughed and spluttered in the dust as the small farm pick-up truck skidded on the dirt road, braking as the driver saw them in the sweep of his lights.

The lights remained on and two men climbed out of the cab, came towards them, and recognising them Shilling Murile waved his bottle and said, chuckling, '*My basies,* there you are. *Sakubona,* boss, I see you.'

'Jesus,' said one of the men. 'These are the bliksems who turned the sheep loose.' He was heavy and red-faced, moustached, and wore clean sports clothes and he was the farm foreman, Opperman. 'Look, this one's actually got a bottle.'

'Shit!' Hannes Meulen swore. 'All the kaffirs are drunk from stealing our wine and those sheep will have to wander about until tomorrow. Where the *donder* they'll land up, I don't know.' He shouted, 'You turned the sheep loose, didn't you?'

'Baas,' the one called Shilling Murile said, 'Nkosizana, young lord, it was to make them dance.'

'*Hulle's dronk.* They're drunk,' Opperman said, standing over the two blacks and glaring down at them. He struck the bottle from Murile's hand and it shattered at the roadside. He looked at Meulen. 'What'll we do? We'll have to take them in to the police-station and lay a complaint.'

'That'll be the day,' Meulen said. 'Today I gave my sister away in marriage and I have guests for the rest of the night. Think you

I'm going to waste time driving all the way to the station? Shit, they can stay here the night, and we'll take them in the morning.'

'Stay here?'

'Have you got something in the lorry to tie them up with? We'll leave them here until morning.'

Opperman walked back to the truck and Meulen, standing in the light of the headlamps, glared at the two ragged men sitting at the roadside. He was wearing wedding clothes and a white carnation had wilted on his lapel. Anger and contempt marred his handsome face with a dark rush of blood and he clenched his fists, shouting, 'Get up, you kaffirs, get up when a white man is near you.'

'Boss,' Shilling Murile said, 'It was to make them dance.'

'I'll give you focken dance.' He turned and went over to the pick-up while Opperman rummaged in the back of it, and reached into the cabin, coming back holding a shotgun. 'Now get up, *bliksem se kaffir*.' He rammed the muzzle of the gun into Murile's face and wagged it at the other one who shivered and sneezed nearby. *'Op, op,* you filth.'

Pain in his cheekbone and the sight of the shotgun sobered him a little, and Shilling Murile dragged himself to his feet, clinging to the fence post, shaking his head, muttering, 'Boss, *is slegte ding,* is a bad thing.'

Opperman was coming from the truck carrying a bundle of electric flex, saying, 'I think this will do.' At the black man he snapped, 'Hold your snout, you have nothing to say, baboon.'

Across the distance the sound of the orchestra still came faintly, mingling with the chirping of crickets, the whisper of the breeze that cut chilly across the fields. Meulen held the shotgun on them and said, 'You kaffirs are getting too smart, first stealing wine and then stealing sheep.' Timi had come partly to his feet, but the liquor made his head pound and his legs would not hold him, and besides that, he was sneezing all the time, his nose running.

Meulen said to his foreman, 'Well, man, tie up those baboons. Fasten them to the posts. They'll be all right here till morning.'

Opperman stared at the two black men, his face suffused with rage because he had to actually touch, handle these kaffirs, and the one who had been doing the talking was saying to Hannes Meulen, 'Baas, you know me. This is a bad thing to do, boss. Why, you know me, I carried the buck which you shot, I cleaned your guns, you know me.'

'Know you shit,' Meulen said with contempt. 'Since when do I know a kaffir? One kaffir looks just like another as it concerns me.' He looked at Opperman, 'Well, *opskut, man,* shake it up.'

Rage made Opperman cruel and he thrust them against the fence posts in turn, while Meulen covered them with the shotgun, lashing them fast with the flex, jerking the bonds tight in his anger so that they cut into flesh, gouged at bone, lashing them to the posts while he cursed them.

The truck backed, made a U-turn and shot away down the farm road sending up an eruption of dust that powdered the two prisoners, then rumbled off into the darkness, its tail-light winking like a red eye through the dust cloud until it was gone.

The two men coughed and choked, wriggling in their bonds. Timi coughed, sneezed and sprayed mucus, moaning as he sagged against the electric flex that held him to the fence post. Shilling Murile wrestled with the flex but Opperman in his rage had been brutally efficient. The rubber-bound wire held them fast, sunk into flesh, clamping the veins, muscles, bones. Struggle against their pinions brought only painful torture, so after a while they gave it up and waited for morning.

The breeze quickened and then a cold wind blew across the country. Night lay wild and deep across the veld and the moonlight was frozen silver that touched but could not dissolve the incredible blackness.

'Utimi, how are you faring?' Shilling Murile asked in the darkness and discovered that he spoke in a croak.

Near him his brother mumbled something which he could not follow: it sounded like something between a choke and a splutter. They could not move; movement brought pain. Afterwards there was only a numbness and muscles and veins and nerves barely functioned as the constricting wire restricted the flow of blood. Near him Shilling Murile heard the sound of painful breathing, the laboured, wheezing sound of a broken pump. His teeth chattered and he shivered with cold. There was a hint of frost in the air as the night moved on and he knew he should stay awake. Shock had sobered him and his mind was clearer, although there was a terrible feeling in his head and he was thirsty.

He said, teeth clicking uncontrollably, 'Listen, brother, do not sleep, do not fall asleep,' but he heard only the tortured wheezing mingled with the sounds of night, the whistle of the wind.

He woke up. He had fallen asleep after all and now he whined and shivered in the stiff, chilled dampness of his ragged shirt and trousers. There was no other feeling over his body except the cold-ness, but his chest burned inside him as if on fire. Nearby he saw the vague form of Timi sagging against the fence post, still and silent.

Gray dawn cracked through the east, followed by a sunless light rushing in across the flat veld that slowly turned pink.

The pick-up truck came rumbling back along the farm road. The sun had not yet dried the damp earth so there was little dust now, and the truck drew slowly to a stop by the fence. Meulen and Opperman climbed out and came over to look at the two scare-crows lashed to the fence posts.

A red spider struggled out of the grass at the roadside and ambled out into the open; Opperman put his foot on it. They were wearing khakis now, Opperman in shorts and shirt with sleeves rolled up, Meulen in bush jacket and slacks. Meulen was smoking a pipe and carrying the shotgun in one hand and he said, 'Well, you had better untie these two baboons.' He did not say anything to the two black men, but merely waited while Opperman dragged a pair of pliers from his hip pocket of his shorts and walked over to the prisoners.

The one called Shilling Murile felt the electric flex give and drop away and he dropped too, falling into the roadway like a dummy; then he heard himself scream with pain as blood started to move through unstopped veins, muscles cracked free, and each unwill-ing pulse brought more pain, more groans. But Timi merely top-pled over and lay in the grass, another dummy bent and twisted in immobile limpness.

Opperman stirred him with a booted foot, bent over and peered at the face, then he looked at Meulen and said, 'God, this one is dead, meneer.'

'Dammit,' Meulen said. 'These kaffirs are always causing trou-ble.'

Lying painfully in the dust of the roadway, Shilling Murile waited for his numbed mind to function. He tried to grasp what he had heard Opperman say and he stared with bloodshot eyes past the two white men to where Timi lay like a broken doll. He was dragging himself painfully to his feet; he wanted to go over to Timi and find out for himself. Staggering to his bare feet he lurched forward and in a hand he was holding the neck of the broken wine bottle with a fearsome spike of glass projecting from it. He heard Meulen cry, '*Pasop*, look out,' and they were turning as he lashed out clumsily.

The spike of bottle-glass slashed the length of Opperman's left forearm, opening it to the bone so that he screamed with pain, staring at the belching blood; Meulen clubbed the black man's skull with the butt of the shotgun.

'*Here ghod*, he almost murdered me,' Opperman yelled and clutched at his elbow, trying to cut off the flood of blood.

In the District Court the charge of sheep-stealing was dropped against the Bantu male, Shilling Murile, but he was charged with the attempted murder of Opperman, found guilty and sentenced to ten years of hard labour.

As for the death of the Bantu Timi, the judge said that there had been provocation. Meneer Meulen had not intended the death of this Bantu, but he should have acted with more thought. Nowadays everybody was very conscious of the necessity to show the white people in a good light in relation to the black population, and Meneer Meulen's actions did not help. Inside the country certain liberalistic elements and Communists would capitalise on such mishaps as this, and overseas the enemies of the country like the Communists there as well as the OAU and the United Nations would also take advantage of such events for their attacks. Meneer Meulen was a well-liked and well-known figure in the local community and should have known better. The judge had no alternative but to render a severe reprimand and a stiff fine.

★

Beyond the door of the hut the sounds of the village mingled with the plaintive bleating of the few sheep in the kraal nearby. Everybody seemed to be busy with something, and there were lights in the houses. A woman called, a dog yap-yapped, somebody was talking hoarsely, and the crickets clicked away in the darkness. It was a hot night and different from the day only because the sun had gone and the actual temperature had dropped a little, but darkness was like a heavy blanket, thick and cloying, raising sweat and turning eyes heavy. The moon was a glowing disc, as if it had taken the place of the sun to scorch the earth at night, and the stars burned like faraway fires.

The shepherd's hut was a round corbelled affair of piled stone of the old times, and the gaps on the wall served a purpose now. The floor of beaten earth was hollowed in the middle where the cold ashes of a fire lay under a blackened saucepan and Madonele ate stiff maize porridge from it with a wooden spoon. He had discarded his blanket and felt hat, and in the light of a half-burned candle on a stone, with his scrawny body and wizened face, the crop of white hair and shrivelled ears, he looked elfin, crouched at the saucepan.

'You should eat,' he piped, gesturing at another spoon sticking out of the stiff porridge.

'I am not hungry,' the man who was called Shilling Murile said. He was still barefoot and was mending a lace in one of his thick boots.

'There is enough,' the shepherd said. 'The woman gives me a few hands of flour because I watch the sheep, but it is hard times with the corn not growing and the *umlungu* at the store not giving credit. How can one sell corn to the dealer if there is none? Only those who have men working in the city can buy something, although now that terrible woman, Mma-Tau, says there are hard times in the cities too and trouble.'

'She seems to know much,' Shilling Murile said.

'She gets letters from the city, and of course she has been there herself. Have you seen the city?'

'A little of it. Lots of things happen there and a man should find it of interest.'

'Will you go there?'

Shilling Murile shrugged his heavy shoulders and tested the strength of the bootlace between his callused hands. 'Who knows?' he said. 'I might go there after I have finished here.'

'Eat something,' Madonele the shepherd said again.

'You eat, madala,' the other said. 'You look as if you need it.'

'I am old and need little', the shepherd said, scraping his spoon clean on the edge of the saucepan. 'An old man like me doesn't need much.'

'Except tobacco,' Shilling Murile said and grinned briefly, He threaded the lace through the eyelets of one of the boots, 'There are some sheep left to be eaten.'

'Aibo, the woman will not allow it, they are to be kept.'

'The woman? Mma-Tau?'

'Who else? She is a power here, above even Hlangeni. It must be because if these few sheep are eaten there will be nothing to breed for wool when the rain comes again. During this drought sheep died and those and others were eaten, because it was needful, but what is to happen when the herd is gone?'

'These may die too. What then?'

Against the wall of the hut the shepherd's old hound looked up

78

and growled in its throat, the scarred head turned towards the door. Against the cicada-sounds outside they heard footfalls on the dry ground, then the woman's voice boomed in the night: 'Ha, inside, let me see you.'

'It is Mma-Tau herself,' the shepherd said, his shrivelled face frowning. 'What would she want with me? To scold me for something, no doubt. But she could have left it until morning, the she-lion.'

'Come out,' the voice bawled. 'Do you think a woman of my size can fit into such a tiny and miserable den?'

'I'll go,' Shilling Murile said and rose to his feet to go bent through the doorway, while Madonele stilled the dog.

Outside the moonlight turned the thorn trees into silhouettes of intricate lace-work. In the kraal up the nearby slope the sheep stirred and rustled. Below, the bustle continued among the houses. Coming out into the moonlight Shilling Murile saw the woman's shape, huge and heavy against the far purple of the sky, blotting out stars and making a dark broad hole in the night.

'There you are,' she said. 'It is you I came for, not that miserable scarecrow of a shepherd. Sakubona, I see you,'

'Kunjani, Mma-Tau,' Shilling Murile said.

'You know me?'

'Who could forget the she-lion?'

The woman laughed, a deep sound, but breathed hard, and flashed small white teeth. She came forward ponderously, her eyeballs gleaming in the dark patch of her face; now he could see her, the vast dress like a tent and the leather belt, the massive arms.

She said, 'It was a walk up this hill; I am not as nimble as I used to be.' She looked around and found a rock, walked over to it and sat down. 'There, let me rest.' The great face shone in the moonlight and she smiled with the wide mouth. 'I saw you going to the graveyard with the shepherd and recognised you at once.' She looked to where Madonele appeared in the doorway of the hut, peering out and said, 'Go away, shepherd, before I crack you like a flea, it is this young man I've come to see.'

'What could you want with me?' Shilling Murile asked, looking suspicious.

The woman leaned her vast hands on huge knees. 'Why, you are of this village. But it is a long time since you played your pranks here, eh? A long time since tying cans to the tails of dogs and stealing eggs. But why should I not welcome you back? It is bad fortune that we do not have any fat calves to slaughter for you, as the Bible says.'

'You think I have come back?' Shilling Murile asked. He sat down against the wall of the hut, looking at the woman with hard eyes. 'I came to visit a grave before going my way.'

'Ah, yes, we are great people for our ancestors, dead relations, brothers, sisters. Well, seeing you from afar, walking with that miserable shepherd, I thought, So he has come back and it is not merely to look at his brother's grave; those two were too close for him to leave it at that, so somebody is going to have trouble.'

'Trouble?'

'I have this nose for smelling out things,' the woman said seriously. 'Listen to me, they say revenge is sweet. Is that it, the sweetness of revenge?'

'What is it to you? It is a debt,' Shilling Murile told her. 'Somebody owes a debt.'

'Certainly,' Mma-Tau said. 'There are many debts to be collected. It is not for me to stand in your way if you wish to collect your debt, but hear this. A whole people is starting to think of collecting a collective debt, the time for collecting this debt is drawing on. All over the country people are feeling it. You have been away for years so you do not know how the porridge is boiling in the pot. In relation to that, your debt, though important to you, becomes of small significance.'

'It is my thing,' Shilling Murile said morosely. 'Wasn't my brother killed?'

'Who is denying that? You are entitled to justice.'

'I have been eight years in the white man's prison.'

'Of course, man. But our people go to prison every day. Are not our leaders in prison? We are all in prison, the whole country is a prison. Our people die all the time, of starvation diseases, of murder, of shooting and hanging.'

'Why are you telling me this?'

'You can be of use to us. You have hatred, strong hatred, the desire to find justice. But do not be satisfied with your personal achievement of justice, if you find it. It is a small thing when compared with the people's need for justice. As I have said, a man with your desire for vengeance belongs with the people.'

Shilling Murile scowled at her. 'I have no need of people. This is my thing, and afterwards I'll go my way.'

'Where will you go?'

'Anywhere.'

'Do you have a pass? Permission to go here, there?'

'I am not concerned with the white man's laws any more. I will go as I please without their pieces of paper.'

The woman laughed, the great body shaking in the moonlight. 'There, you see? You have the spirit of defiance.' She shook her head. 'Ai, these passes, needed for moving here, moving there. I remember when they were first forced upon women. I was one of those who marched to the capital to protest. Thousands of women, and it gave a sense of power. One learned the power of numbers.'

'You seem to be dangerous woman,' he said. 'You should be in the city, not here.'

She laughed again. 'Bah, they found me to be too dangerous for the city, so I am here. I went there to be a nurse and they decided otherwise. It is strange, how they set a trap for themselves each time. One becomes too troublesome in the city, so they send one to the countryside, so one becomes troublesome in the countryside. Doesn't the countryside have grievances? They send home work-less men who starve in the city to starve in the country. So we will work to join the people of the country with those of the city. It is a trap they find themselves in each time, and one day the trap will snap shut eh?'

'You are a dangerous woman, for the sister of a chief,' Shilling Murile said. He did not want to give any thought to what she was saying, but he listened out of basic politeness, not wishing to offend her.

'The sister of a chief,' she said heavily, sitting in the night gloom with her vast hands on her knees. 'He is not an unkind man, and he is not like you. He is satisfied with government's pieces of paper. He obeys the law, you see, and they have noticed this. Why, even when he was demoted to headman, they continued to pay him a stipend. He is grateful, so he remains obedient. Why was he demoted? They did not trust him.'

'He should know better,' Murile said in his morose tone. 'He went to school, many years.'

'School!' she said, and laughed. 'Yes, and I went to school too. Together we used to walk six miles to and from school which you know was at the mission. Perhaps the school did not teach him to be a chief.' She shook her head. 'Still, he is my brother and there is hope for him. He even went to a college.'

'You have lived in the city too.'

The woman laughed again and quivered all over. 'What a place a city is; all that activity, that rushing back and forth, and the things one did there. Yes, the city was a good place to be, in spite of everything.' She reminisced again, gazing past the hut against which Murile sat, out into the starlit darkness. 'I belonged to *Ukongo* and to a lodge while I was there. When I had to leave to return here they gave a *stokfel*, the people who knew me. Hauw, what a stokfel that was. It lasted all night and the whole of the next day. A crowd came, people coming and going all the time — I lived in a local township. Each time anybody wished to partake in the stokfel he or she paid something. For instance when one wished someone to dance, he put something in the plate; there was a band and they did not play until those had contributed. Or if somebody wanted to drink, or relate some anecdote or story, or tell a joke, each event required a coin or two. Of course when a lot of beer and brandy had been consumed and everybody became merry and talkative, or wished to dance, that was when the money came in. Hauw, there was singing and dancing and speeches, you know how an indaba can go on for time without end — and once a couple of *tsotsis* tried to start a fight, but I handled them well. One old man, I think his name was Molwene, told a story about a crocodile which went on a long time. I forget the story, but it provoked much protesting by those present who wished to tell their own things. After a while he was compelled to stop and he left saying it was not proper to force a man to end his discourse before he reached the end. The speeches and story-telling happened in the yard, while the dancing took place inside. That was an occasion to remember, and when it was over it was spoken about for a long time, as those who wrote to me afterwards said. The money went to Ukongo, the organisation, and I might tell you . . . But there, I am rambling like a senile old woman. What were we talking about beforehand?'

Shilling Murile thought, she is certainly rambling, and I did not come all this way to listen to such palaver; I must be going. But the woman was saying, 'Ah, yes, we were talking of Hlangeni, my brother.' Her tongue made a clucking sound and her voice was serious. 'My brother, and there is a shamefulness about him. Why, when the Bantu Commissioner came here with his paper with the names of all to be moved, and a man with a can of paint, was it not my brother, Hlangeni, who took them around pointing out houses where each on the list lived? The man with the paint put a mark on the door while Hlangeni watched. It is true to say he appeared shamed, but it was his co-operation that was most shameful.'

'What will you do?' Shilling Murile asked reluctantly. He did not wish to become involved, but curiosity urged him. 'I heard you say that nobody would obey.'

The woman gestured about her with huge arms, pointing into the darkness. 'All this was our land, since the time of our ancestors. In that my brother was right. Are not the fields still ours, the soil, the hills? All that is our home, in spite of the white man's law. Listen, we have a committee and the committee spoke and decided.'

'What about your brother? He knows of your committee? It undermines his authority.'

The vast shoulders shrugged mountainously. 'Perhaps he does, perhaps he does not. It is a secret, but who can say that some woman or old man has not prattled? Still, if he knows and revealed it, the government would have been here already. Perhaps he knows and knows also that to yap like a hyena about it would be an additional shame, and I think that Hlangeni's shoulders grow tired with the burden of shame.' She looked at him, the whites of her eyes pronounced in the broad face. 'But there, I have told you too, but then I don't have any doubts about you. You are of us, even if you deny it, because of your own special hatred for them.' She chuckled and the huge body shook again, the small white teeth flashing in the moonlight. 'You are not a bad fellow. Very sulky, but not bad. If you think ...'

She stopped because the hound had started growling again inside and there were the sounds of snapping twigs and rustling undergrowth and a child, a girl in a torn dress, hair in tight plaits, came out of the gloom to where they talked.

'Ah, girl, what is it?' Mma-Tau asked, her voice soft with the child.

'Mma-Tau mama, it is *Ausi* Tsoane.'

The woman rose ponderously, raised her thick hands. '*Yoh*, why should she start now? I am coming, child.' She looked at Shilling Murile while the child disappeared into the darkness. 'It is a woman in labour.' She shook her head and clucked, then said drily: 'Her husband works in the city. With great consideration the law allows a woman to go without permission into the white city for seventy-two hours, in order to conceive. Such was the case with Mrs Tsoane. Well, let me go and help bring forth whatever she intends.' Turning to the door of the hut, her voice boomed again: 'Madonele, old man, do not forget your task.'

The shepherd appeared in the doorway and bowed towards her. 'Never, Mma-Tau, never.' The white hair gleamed in the moonlight as he bobbed his head rapidly. 'Everything shall be as you ordered.'

A heavy hand slapped the shoulders of Shilling Murile who had risen to his bare feet. 'Well, I must leave you now, and it is possible that we shall not meet. Then again . . .' She shook her great head and then smiled with the small white teeth. 'Go well, *madoda*. You're not a bad young man.'

When she was gone, walking heavily off into the darkness and down to where the rest of the village seemed still to be bustling under the stark trees, Shilling Murile turned back into the shepherd's hut. The candle had burned down low and the circular area was in heavy gloom. He sat down near the light and brushed dust from his feet while the shepherd crouched down again, watching him.

'You are going now?' the shepherd asked, sounding a little plaintive.

'We will have a smoke together first,' Shilling Murile said pulling on his boots.

'That she-lion talks too much,' Madonele said, and giggled thinking of tobacco. 'Do this and do that. Why has this not been done? Why has that not been done? Hauw, she roars all the time.'

'She trumpets like a she-elephant,' the other said. 'And is as big as one.'

'Aai, what a woman. Did you like what she said?'

'I did not listen very carefully,' Shilling Murile said. Looking away, he drew tobacco and the brown paper from his battle blouse. 'I have matters of my own to attend to.'

He looked defiantly at the shepherd again, waiting to be contradicted, but Madonele remained silent, turning his little raisin eyes away, a thin hand scratching the back of the old hound lying by him. Murile sat on his haunches and rolled a cigarette. He licked it carefully into shape and then passed the packet of tobacco to the shepherd who received it in cupped hands, thanking him politely, trying not to appear too eager. He filled his pipe in silence passing the tobacco back, leaving the other to relish his own dark thoughts again, and now Shilling Murile rose restlessly to his feet, saying, 'I am wasting time here, old man. The night draws on and it is time that I went.'

'I am sorry,' the shepherd said simply.

Shilling Murile looked at him for a moment, his eyes screwed up against the cigarette smoke. Then he shrugged his heavy shoulders and went out through the low doorway of the hut, carrying the old army blouse.

'Go well through *isango elikle*,' the shepherd murmured in the small light of the dwindling candle. 'Through the good gate.'

He pulled on the army blouse and wriggled his big shoulders inside it. Around him the night hung hot and starlit, the faraway moon rolling across the dark sky like a yellow marble from a giant's hand. Near him the crickets made their tiny clamour and the fires still burned here and there in the little village. His heavy boots made soft grating sounds as he set off through the powdery sand and the dry and scanty grass. Madonele the shepherd crouched in the hut and heard him go, one thin dusty hand gently scratching the dog's back while the other clasped the long-stemmed, tall-bowled pipe at which he sucked contemplatively, staring ahead. Later, when the candle flickered he turned his snow-capped head towards it and saw in its light that Shilling Murile had left the half-empty bag of tobacco.

*

The ceiling of hardboard sagged and there were cracks in it, yet it was a ceiling. There was an old sideboard with wrought metal handles to the doors and drawers, and porcelain ornaments on top of it, with a cut glass bowl filled with dusty plastic flowers. On the whitewashed wall over the sideboard was a big, faded photograph in a chipped gold-leaf frame of a man dressed in what looked like an admiral's uniform of the last century. This was Hlangeni's father who had once been received by the then Governor General. There was also a smaller picture of Hlangeni as a young man.

Hlangeni huddled in an old armchair not unlike a throne, but this was not the young Hlangeni of the picture, posing beside the tall pedestal and the potted palm. He had removed his jacket and now had an old *kaross* of goatskin wrapped about his fallen shoulders; he had brought the paraffin lamp with the brass base, which had been in the family since the time of his mother, to the little ornamental table beside him. The light from the lamp caused his white hair to glow, but did not illuminate the look of ire, worry and sullenness in the tobacco-leaf eyes. His dark fingers plucked at the hair of the skin cape and the eyes stared straight ahead out of folds of collapsed flesh into the gloom beyond the dining-table with the water carafe. Doors led to other parts of the house and from beyond the curtained window came the sound of voices mingling with the singing of crickets and the whack-whack-whack of an axe. Hlangeni wondered what work could be going on in the dark.

After a while, the front door opened to let in a glimpse of starlit night and the smell of woodfires, then it was filled by the wide bulk of his sister's form; raising his eyes Hlangeni saw her small white teeth gleaming in the half-light as she asked, shutting the door again: 'Am I allowed to enter?'

'You are in already,' he said a little sharply, and then his gaze dropped. 'You come and go as you please, say as you please.'

She came forward heavily, her man's boots clumping on the rammed earth floor. 'That woman Tsoane has given birth to twins. Twins at this time of her and our lives. And she with a husband in the city.'

Hlangeni muttered, 'Twins. There was a time when everybody would rejoice at the birth of twins. Now they are just two more future followers of your nonsense.'

She went and sat ponderously on a sofa near him. 'Well, we shall have to leave her and her babes here with you.'

'Must I watch over babes?'

'And old men,' the woman said gruffly. 'It is what you are fit for. Perhaps the newborn will grow up to become faithful followers of you. Who knows? The woman naturally cannot go with us, so she will stay with the others who do not wish to follow.'

He looked at her sitting there encircled by her man's belt, and his mouth curled. 'You will lead them all to hell, you will.'

She said heavily, 'Listen, it is better to retain dignity in hell than to be humiliated in their heaven. Nevertheless, if they want to throw us out let them come and chase us all over the hills first.'

'What is all that chopping?' Hlangeni asked. His fingers continued to worry the kaross.

'Barricades,' his sister answered. 'We won't let their lorries in here.'

'It is foolishness,' Hlangeni said, his tone suddenly angry. 'What good does it do?'

She said sadly, her eyes on her brother: 'Come, show a little courage. Your ancestors led our people with spears against their guns.'

'They were destroyed,' he said, his voice sullen again.

'Defeated perhaps, but not destroyed. You know that. One day we will have guns too.'

The lamp smoked and let off a smell of burning oil. She reached out with a huge hand and turned down the wick. 'Foolishness,' Hlangeni repeated in the diminished light. 'It is the nonsense you learned in the city. Why did you not stay there? You are an evil spirit.'

'They expelled me, as you know.' She gazed into the darkness across the room as if she saw something there. 'Still, it was good in the city in many ways. I miss the noise and everything that goes with it.' For a while she had a faraway look, lost in thought, peering into a kaleidoscope of memories.

She was in a train, a long string of third-class carriages, rumbling its way through the suburbs, packed as usual with the great crowd of black workers being carried towards the locations and townships outside the city. They packed the hard wooden seats and the aisles, overflowed onto the window-sills, backsides jutting into space. The more daring rode the couplings, clinging to every projection. The train swayed dangerously and inside the carriages the passengers were continuously hurled against each other, struggling to maintain their balance, clawing each other, cursing and laughing, faces bright with perspiration in the sweltering air trapped there with them, rank with the smell of armpits, feet, bodies. The train hurtled past the suburbs, the neat cottages with trim hedges, tiled roofs, now and then a big house or a mansion with glittering windows, lawns, and flowerbeds. Then the suburbs gave way to waste land, the municipal dump, a scrapyard piled with the wreckage of motor vehicles like the detritus of war. The train lost speed as it came up to stretches of tumbledown shacks and shanties huddled together as if clutching each other to avoid falling down. The evening sun glinted off tin roofs, sparkled on drums of water under topsy-turvy outhouses. Then all this slipped away and the swaying carriages, with the sound of rapid fire, broke through acres and acres split with rows and rows of similar two-roomed breeze-block boxes, ranks of metal or asbestos roofs waiting in close formation, monotonous grey and dispassionately geometric under the unwashed curtain of smoky haze that hung in the twilight air.

Between the platforms of the featureless station the carriage-doors burst open like wounds and from them people erupted in dark gouts to stream towards the exits, screaming with relief, laughter soaked up by the padding of a multitude of feet hurrying to get to what was home before the darkness fell.

Another woman with a bag stuffed with rummage jostled her, and ahead a man in tattered overalls, balancing a load of planks on a shoulder, whistled and shouted at those in front to give way. Everybody was in a hurry and rushed past her bulk like water around a boulder.

There was no check for pass-books this time and the crowd broke from the station to scatter into the ghetto under the impersonal eyes of a pair of duty policemen who sat in the cabin of a Land Rover, windows armoured with thick wire mesh, while a black constable with a spear lounged against the fender outside.

She said a jocular hello to the man with the spear and passed the police patrol, moving on with the gush of people up a street between rows of identical cubes. She was one of the crowd, she was going home to one of these cubes with the dusty patches in front of the doors, the stick-and-wire fences, the pathways bordered with scraps of slate or up-ended jam tins, soot and grime collecting at the corners and the walls already cracking in places.

Among those on their way from the station, there were others moving aimlessly, tugged at by toddlers with naked bellies. Older urchins in clothes too big for their bodies, cut down from the cast-offs of parents, bought at a jumble sale. The crowd milled about like refugees brought from a flood or an earthquake waiting for the promised relief.

She belonged with the tiredness, the laughter, the home-coming to the fried dough, the watery tripe, sour porridge. the slabs of yesterday's bread, the patchwork children behind the fences, the smell of smoke in the dusty yards.

They are getting tired of it, she thought. Tired of the tiredness, the everlasting penny-pinching, the perpetual raids for licences to live. A hungry man walked into a delicatessen in the city in broad daylight and grabbed a chicken, walked out and devoured it on the sidewalk, in full view of the gawping customers and the counter-man. They are getting tired of hunger, she thought. They spoke about it in the smutty canteens of factories, around the gates, in the yards, over fences, in meetings; daubed it on walls in bleeding paint.

'A chief should be obeyed.' Hlangeni said, interrupting her thoughts and bringing back the sound of crickets, the thumping of axes.

She looked at him from the sofa which her great body almost filled, looming in the dark. He was huddled in his armchair, the restless hands fiddling, as if trying to pluck dignity, pride, from the goatskin cape, the collapsed face trembling with an effort to appear stately, and she said, not unkindly, 'A chief yes, even though you submitted without protest when they reduced you to a headmanship. You let them do it. First they allow you some authority over your people, then they take it away. Yet you speak of being obeyed.'

'Times have changed.'

'Eweh, times have changed. Before a chief listened to the voices of his councillors. Then *they* came and used the chief only as a whip over the people. Now your people say, if the chief is only a whip, let us cast him aside.'

'I keep them out of trouble.'

'Trouble? Have we not always had trouble?'

'They are giving us new land,' he muttered hopelessly.

'New land? You have seen this new land. Does the grass grow there? Are our ancestors buried there? Will you visit the graves of our father and mother there? Perhaps you will want to come back here to meditate over our father who was a chief too. You will have to go to them and ask their permission. Humbly. You will say, Please, great lord, I wish to visit a grave, give me a piece of paper that will carry me there. And you talk of being a chief.' She hauled herself up angrily, struggling to raise her great weight. When she was upright she looked down on him, a little breathless. 'Show a little courage,' she said. 'Just a little courage.'

Clumping over to the door, she placed a vast hand on the latch and looked back at him. His form danced in the flicker of the lamp's flame. She said, opening the door after a while, 'I have ordered the shepherd to take all the sheep to the hills.' Before going out she looked back again at the old man crouched in the gloom. 'It is strange,' she said frowning, 'them praying for rain. I remember when they used to mock us when we sang the rain songs.'

★

The moon lay like a silver coin flicked onto the black cloth of the sky, and the stars had now receded into the darkness. A certain coolness pervaded the air, easing the heat of the night a little. Around the old, crumbling homestead the crickets still combined their little sounds into a discordant nightsong. The moon was motionless; only in the brittle grass some night insects stirred, and the farm-hound pricked up its ears in the space where it had come awake, between ground level and the floor of the old house which was raised on corner-stones. A growl rumbled in its throat. A footstep crackled on gravel and the hound rose silently, sniffing, watching. The footsteps stopped. There was only darkness, but the man-smell was there and the hound charged, fangs bared as its barking tore the night.

In the big old-fashioned bed the old man tossed and mumbled in sleep, protesting over disturbed dreams. In the old thatch the rats moved and scrabbled, the beams winced and creaked with age and the temperature, while bundled under blankets even in this warm night, the old man's ancient, decaying body shifted, fragile bones seeking further warmth as life seeped unseen from it. The tooth-less old mouth mumbled in the parchment-dry, withered face as the hound yapped somewhere out beyond the dreams, the old mud walls, the overhanging eaves, the harsh and tussocked grass.

In a half-dream he saw now that he was a boy again and that the hound, another hound then, circled restlessly around where he saw himself sitting mounted with the other old riders in the high grass. They were rough men, bearded and smelling of leather and sweat, their rifles unslung from their shoulders where the straps had worn the hide or cord jackets, carrying them across their saddle-bows now, eyes watchful under the floppy brims of their old felt hats. Earlier they had shot a buck now slung across the back of a spare horse led by the boy.

Before them the undulating plain scattered away towards the horizon that was all yellow grass. They sat their mounts and watched the land, the boy with them, small on his bay, holding the lead-rope of the pack horse and the hounds fretful in the grass about the fetlocks. Somewhere far behind was the settlement, the trade store, the zinc-roofed houses. They were passing through from the east and they'd brought the boy along because though he could shoot and ride he needed more experience, craft, wiliness.

One of the men spat a chew of tobacco aside and said, 'Old Bushman country; they are somewhere out there. They were pushed into the desert long ago, but they still hunt this far.'

Nobody made comment; they were a quiet people, given rather to harsh practicalities than unnecessary conversation. Conversation was for the camp-fire, the stoeps of homesteads, celebrations. The land was settled now except for scanty frontiers where the restless ones ranged.

A long way ahead a herd of *wildebeest* broke the horizon and raced towards the east, the sound of their hooves carrying like faraway drums. The boy sat on his horse and watched the far-off dark line of the herd grinding the grass flat. He wore a stiff new beaver hat.

Then suddenly the two dogs were away, dashing from the group of riders towards the rear and a series of undulating, grass-grown hills.

'Back!' the tobacco-chewing man yelled, 'Back!' They all tried to turn their mounts, the horses bumping and pushing each other, and the man was yelling, 'Spread out, spread out, men.'

Somebody said, 'Ah!' and slumped from his saddle with the tiny arrow sticking out below a shoulder-blade. Shocked, the boy dropped the lead-rope of the pack horse and they fanned out while arrows fell in the grass nearby. The rifles came up to their shoulders, single-action breech-loaders, the sun-creased eyes sighting carefully along the barrels, and the boy, heart fluttering, his eyes screwed along the length of the weapon beyond the breech, saw the tiny figures in the long grass, the little bows bent. The hounds were dead in the spiky grass a distance away.

The little bows twitched — it was too far for the sound of their strumming to be heard — and the horsemen fired at the same time, half of them, while the rest charged, and they reloaded.

The boy saw the tiny naked figures fleeing into the tall grass and the riders who had gone ahead circle — aiming, firing. Little figures bobbed and rolled and jerked in the grass. The rest of the commando, the boy with them, spurred past those who were now loading, ramming the bullets home, searching the grass, passing the shot bodies of the little men in loin-cloths and cloaks of springbok hide; then suddenly parallel to them, on each flank, the little figures rose again and this time the boy heard the twang of the bows. A horse went down with a snort and squeal, turning belly over head taking its rider with it, crushing him; another bearded and bandoliered man fell backward from his saddle. But now the others were firing into the darting little band of near-naked men. They were hardly taller than children, the boy saw, as they dropped squirming under the heavy slugs. Some of them got away into the bush country and the tobacco-chewing man shouted for his men, calling off the chase.

The horse that had fallen was dead, hit in the withers by a poisoned arrow, and its rider was dead too with a crushed spine and shattered legs. The first man took an hour, the poison from the tip of the little arrow taking that long to do its work.

'*Duiwel*,' the tobacco-chewing leader said, spitting again. 'They made that herd run to distract us. They were hunting this way and saw us.'

'They killed the dogs,' the boy said sadly.

One of the men turned over a tiny body with his veld-boot, ignoring the spilled intestines, while the boy vomited on the grass, seeing the little sightless eyes, a necklace made from pieces of ostrich-shell about the limp neck. '*Daar*,' the man said, grimacing at the shaking boy. 'To remind you of your little skirmish.'

'I thought they'd all been driven off long ago,' one of the other men said. 'Little devils with their poison arrows.

The dead men lay under mounds in the long yellow grass and the tobacco-chewing man had read the burial service from the old Bible he carried in his saddle-bag with the biltong and coffee; afterwards, when they set off again with the buck's carcass on the pack horse and leading the spare horses, the tobacco-chewing commandant posted outriders as scouts and the boy was glad he was chosen as one of them so they could not see his shaky paleness and trembling hand tugging at the brim of his beaver hat. He remembered the sightless little eyes. The main group was talking of possible war against the Englanders, in between commiserating over the death of their three companions.

The old mind, cluttered with rummage, bits and pieces of life stored in the cobwebby cupboards of his feeble brain that now and then projected them in some sort of order, sank back into a black quagmire of sleep. Death lurked, waited in the gloom beyond the foot of the bed, patient with the old man's stubbornness to die, allowing him now and then the scanty luxury of dreams, as if a few more fleeting images on the stained and tattered screen of memory would generously compensate for the coming eternity of silence.

Now huddled in the big, rumpled bed, groping for warmth, he remembered, partly comatose with sleep, 'They killed the dogs.'

Perhaps it had been the last yelp of the hound outside which had stirred this memory. As it dashed from the shelter of the old homestead into the dooryard, the hands of the one they called Shilling Murile clamped skilfully about its throat and cut off the barking, holding on tightly, squeezing while the animal clawed and thrashed and its neck finally snapped.

Pale and warm moonlight lay in the dooryard around the crumbling house the Oupa had built so many years ago. The rats wriggled in the rotting, overhanging eaves, the ruins of the grass armchair disintegrated on the stoep — the old man was far too feeble now to sit out there. Beyond the furrowed and hollowed yard the broader area fronting the New House a short distance away was carefully laid out with plants and bushes, flowers, all washed by moonlight.

The New House was built to the plan of an H. Many of the original homesteads formed a T, but here a wing had been added at the back, with straight side gables, two-storeyed with the bedrooms above, and below the vast kitchen and pantry. From the front one ascended the front stoep, polished red, and faced a gable in the baroque style; at the sides were gables of the concave-convex style. One entered through teak entrance doors which had side windows into the large entrance-way, the *voorhuis*, or hall, which led towards the rear, but screened with ornate stinkwood. On the right was the great lounge where the guests would be received and leading to the dining-room. On the other side was the owner's study — he was standing for parliament — his library — one had to subscribe to Hansard and the statute books — and the new gunroom, for he would still go hunting.

The Niewehuis stood silent and deserted in the white moonlight that reflected off the many-paned windows upstairs. Somewhere in the surrounding darkness the night insects chirped away and in the sagging old bed the old man gobbled like a turkey in his sleep and cough-cough-coughed on phlegm.

'Let me go to him,' Koos whimpered hearing the feeble sounds inside. Shrivelled and small as a pygmy, his monkey-face lost in the dark and only the white peppercorn hair showing here and there, he writhed in the grip of the big man whose great hand bunched up the ragged old overcoat he wore.

'Go to him!' the man called Shilling Murile sneered. 'Slave, I should wring your little neck as I did the dog's.'

'He was the old master's dog, he was very old, now he is dead.'

'As you all should be,' the big man growled in the darkness and shook the old retainer in his clamped hand as if rattling a gourd. Having heard the hound's last yelp, Koos had emerged from behind the old homestead where he slept in the kitchen, to be seized suddenly by a hand that came out of the darkness, and now he whined, 'You'll not make *him* dead? Not the *oubaas*?'

'Oubaas. You and your oubaas. Say rather your lord and master, you slave, for have you not been his slave all these years?'

Behind the dark window of the mouldering house the old man coughed phlegm, and Koos whispered: 'He'll die soon, anyway. There have been too many years for him and for me too. It is time to die, aai, it is time to die, but let him die in peace.'

'Yes, and you will sit by your master's bedside, ja, and watch him die, slave, and you will weep over him,' Murile said. Something stirred inside him and he gripped the shivering Koos brutally, almost strangling the ancient retainer with the collar of the old overcoat. 'You'll be a slave to the end? Don't you think of the things they did? To your people?' The word lay unfamiliar on his tongue, a taste long forgotten and now remembered with difficulty.

'It was a long time ago; one forgets. Besides, he was kind.' Hands, dry and brittle as sapless twigs, scratched feebly at the big man's arm. 'What do you look for here? There's nothing here.'

Murile chuckled humourlessly. 'I did not come all this way to wring the necks of a pair of juiceless roosters. Tell me, slave, is your young lord, the nkosizana, sleeping in his beautiful house?'

'He is in the town. I believe he'll return tomorrow at sunset. In the town he stays at the white people's hotel.'

'And that Opperman?'

'He is dead some years now.'

'Dead, eh? Perhaps he is lucky. Then there is nobody at home?'

'Nobody.' The toothless mouth mumbled reluctantly, 'There's nothing to take either. A lot of new furniture, ja, but nothing one could carry. When the young — uh — master marries, there will be many new and pretty things.'

'Dog, slave,' Murile said in the dark of the dooryard. 'You take me for a common thief?' He grinned as if he found something humorous about the past, his teeth shining in the moonlight. 'Why, don't you remember? I used to work here many years ago.'

'I sensed that I know you from somewhere, remembered you,' Koos mumbled. He looked anxiously toward the dark window of the old house, while Murile said:

'Think, did I not help to make the farm a good one? Did I not also scurry about the young boss's heels? I used to carry his guns when he went hunting. I was a boy then.'

'You went away,' the wrinkled mummy-face gabbled. 'Why have you come back?'

'To see the places of my boyhood, fool. Should a man not see the place of his youth again? Would you like to see the place of your boyhood, old man? Not you, because you are a slave following everywhere in the footsteps of your master, even to the grave. But I, I have come all this way to be with . . . ' Something stirred within him again and he muttered, 'To see my people.' Then his mood changed and he growled, his face close to the shrivelled mask above the bunched overcoat. 'There, I came to see this fine place I left behind years ago, as you know. No doubt the young lord, the Boer, still keeps many of his things there, like the guns he hunted with? The mounted heads of the kudu? Just to see them, to look at them, to remember how I walked behind, carrying them.'

'I should get a beating if it was found out I let you in. I am trusted with the keys; I clean up, sweep, dust. But to let you in could mean a beating.' The wrinkled face puckered like a child's and tears sprang from it.

'Bah!' Shilling Murile said. 'And I could snap thy neck like a twig and who would then be at the bedside of your revered oubaas when he dies? And I could take the keys from your pocket and burn the house down. That would be a sight, wouldn't it? For miles around.' He giggled. 'We could have a braaivleis, hey?'

The old servant moaned and inside the tumbledown homestead, behind the dark and shuttered windows, the sagging stoep, the old man coughed again and mumbled in his sleep, 'Karel, *ach*, Karel, I am sorry. Should I pray?' It was strange that Karel should be wearing the suit he had worn as best man at the old man's wedding. Only his face did not rejoice but was dead and his eyes were the little, blank sightless eyes staring up from the bloody, tussocky grass, and there was a necklace of ostrich-shells about his neck.

Then the old man woke up in the dark and remembered it all clearly: Karel, his old friend, lying angled amid the outcroppings on the hillside that was part of the north-east face of what was called Spioonkop. He had really been wearing coarse corduroys and a speckled waistcoat under the crossed bandoliers, only the clothes did not seem to fit him properly now that he was bundled untidily and dead from the Lee-Metford bullet in his head, the fair hair bloody. There were more dead along the slope, but the old man, who was young and a commando soldier then, did not notice them, weeping over his friend and seeing through his tears trickling into his new, clipped beard, the staring, sightless eyes that seemed to remind him even then of something out of the past. He said, choking: 'Karel, *ach* Karel, I am sorry, sorry. Should I pray?' It did not matter to him then that there was fighting up and down the hillside, while he muttered the prayer in the Dutch as they'd always been taught, until the *veldkornet* dragged him away, urging him up the hill again into the fire from the Lancashire Fusiliers.

Now the old man remembered how he and Karel had been together through most of the campaigns against the British, remembering in the dark room with the splinters of moonlight lingering like the waiting fingers of featureless death. He waited tiredly for death to come, to reach out, and thought how he had faced death in the past — he and old Karel.

Modderriver where they'd laid the trap expertly. They'd crossed the river to the southern bank of the Riet which branched off from the Modder, when the British had expected them to occupy and defend the northern side and the town and roads. Digging the trenches in front of the river bank, the trenches short lengths and irregularly lined, six men to a trench and the parapets concealed with rocks and bushes. They had withstood the British at Eslin Hoogte, bearing the artillery shelling, making the British come on to be mown down. Now here they waited again, entrenched along the southern bank where they had a clear field of fire across the bare veld which sloped gently towards them, while the British artillery would be ranging on what they could see across the river. One did not know what generals thought about — *they* had had Koos de la Rey, and some German advisers and instructors, and the British had had someone called Methuen, they heard. For the rest, they were just there waiting in the trenches below the river, huddled in the night, waiting for sunrise and the enemy.

Early in the burgeoning morning they'd seen the Scots Guards for the first time. They'd chuckled, joked over these soldiers in what they called woman's skirts. There were other troops too, *natuurlik*, but these Scottish were very curious, there in the November morning. The old man recalled that a flock of small birds rose from the veld as they watched the lines of manoeuvring soldiers, these Scotsmen among them.

Unseen, sighting along the Mauser rifles hidden in the camouflage rocks and bushes, thinking come along, *nooientjies*, little ladies, come to the ball.

There were the officers a-horse, riding confidently with their companies, the nailed boots of their men going swish-swish in the grass. Eight hundred yards, closer, closer and then the crash of volley firing and the ground dotted with the dead and the wounded and the remains of *verdomde* Scotsmen trying to make a ridiculous charge into the lethal fire. That was all the old man and Karel knew about the battle. They had been withdrawn amid the crackle of riflery and the clacking of a pom-pom gun somewhere.

But Karel wasn't here any more. Perhaps it was best he never knew they'd lost the war after all. Gay Karel who had been best man at his wedding — and the old man could not cry now, feeling as if all tears had dried in him, an old sweat rag wrung out, and there was only loneliness and the moon-slivered darkness — not even that damned Koos. Koos, where's that Koos? He is never at hand when needed.

★

It was not as if Jaap Opperman really believed in ghosts or spells or such devilish phenomena. But his mother, the late *Tant'* Philipa had done so and, of course, it was natural that some suspicion, at least, that such things might exist, rubbed off on her son. Certainly Tant' Philipa was a Christian, believing fast in the Living God, and went to church regularly until rheumatics caused her attendance to turn sporadic. But she also believed in the Devil and all his works, in witchcraft, spells, curses and ghosts because they were the other side of the spiritual coin, as it were. She was not the only one of her people who believed in such things, and when it came to the special powers of black witch-doctors, medicine-men, diviners, she cast race prejudice aside and did not hesitate to consult one such whenever some affliction assailed her, her family or a valuable cow; or to apply the numerous remedies alleged to have been learned from them at one time or another.

Jaap recalled the time when as a child he had gone down with colic or inflammation of the bowels, and the mother had cured it, or so she insisted, by butchering and skinning a cat and plastering his abdomen with the smoking pelt. One supposed that the virtual plague of fleas escaping from the bloody fur and invading patient, bedding and everything else was to be ignored in favour of the more important cure.

Certainly there might be curative properties in the herbs and simples the old woman gathered, but there were those who felt a little uncomfortable when she claimed that it was possible to foretell the future by peering into the guts of a newly-slaughtered chicken.

When Tant' Philipa herself felt ill or suffered from some ailment indivinable, she would dress in her best and take the train to a place where an important black magician and diviner held his court. Let it be recognised that she was not the only one of the chosen race to come from far and wide to pay tribute, strangely enough, to this respected witch-doctor. Usually his yard was surrounded by parked automobiles bearing the number plates of all points of the compass and thronged with pilgrims, all come to consult the divining bones.

'Don't underestimate the powers of a kaffir,' Tant' Philipa warned. 'They got ways we don't know of. Especially don't do a black no harm. Remember, even dead he will get even.'

After all, if one believed in the power of God, one also had to believe in the heathen mysteries. And blacks particularly must be in league with the Prince of Darkness, otherwise they would not be black.

'A kaffir knows snakes,' she claimed. 'He and the snake, they are friends. Heads under the same blanket, so to say. Besides monkey-tails, you will always find snake skins among the things a clever black keeps. And does the snake not represent the first evil, the Devil in the Garden, that tempted Mother Eve? Ja, a black is a great friend of the snake, mark my words, hoh.'

The Dominee Visser did not hold with this too literal endowment of black people with magical powers, and he stressed that their lack of civilisation and their heathenism was enough to contend with. In the meantime, he tolerated some of the minor superstitions and idiocies among his flock as well as sighing resignedly over the folly of such as Tant' Philipa.

'And keep away from the *Kloof*,' she advised her son.

'What ravine?' the boy asked with curiosity.

'You'll find out where,' she replied. 'You can see it from the deep road, but don't go near there. It is holy ground for the blacks. A big chief or something so was buried up there in olden times and they say his ghost stands guard up there, watching over his people. Not even Oupa Meulen's Hottentot or that shepherd from the kaffir camp goes near. It's no place for them, let alone white folk. So keep away.'

The Kloof, the boy learned, was part of the local folk history. Not that it was any extraordinary kloof: just a cut in the rocky hills seen as a brown scar in the distance, and as the years passed, one could see from a careful stone's throw away, that its entrance became clogged with brush and stunted trees. It had something to do with the wars of dispossession generations back — what the whites called 'The Kaffir Wars' — but what exactly, few could say. Stories abounded, but none of them were ever identical.

Tant' Philipa was always getting about, advising and administering: being driven into the little town by Jaap on Sundays for *nagmaal* or whenever occasion took him there, so she could pass the time with Mrs Kroner who ran the Railway Hotel, and others.

In the meantime the Kloof was always there, the narrow ravine cutting into the hills. It was noted that the blacks themselves never took their cattle grazing in that direction. Little Jaap Opperman looked that way with a certain awe: his mother was probably right about the hex on it. And the black children he played with sometimes made up stories about it. As a child one could associate with black children, but when one grew up it was different — one got to know one's place.

The Oppermans were small farmers — a patch of land, a few cows and sheep, some chickens. After old Opperman had been stomped into the dust by an infuriated bull, the farm had passed to the wife and Jaap. 'Must have been frightened by a snake,' Tant' Philipa said, drying her eyes, and referring to the bull.

Farming interrupted schooling; then later they had found the farm too much and too profitless to run, so it had been sold to the Meulens to be annexed, and young Jaap had accepted paid employment which eventually led to the foremanship of the Meulen estate. It was not a vastly responsible position as all he had to do, really, was to see that the numerous blacks did their work keeping the farm going.

'You treat them strict but right,' Jaap Opperman's mother advised. 'A person never knows what hex they can put on you.' She was ageing and helpless with the dropsy, attended by a maid from the coloured location until she died.

Jaap did not mind having the coloured girl around. She was a heavy-eyed, heavy-hipped she-animal with thick frizzy hair and quivering dugs. As long as one did not openly parade her, she could go unnoticed by most. When sexual consorting with other races was made illegal by the government, it became more complicated. He had to let the girl go back to the location each night to return in the morning. One had to be careful: there were reports in the

newspapers of white men getting into trouble over black women —
even suicides.

'You keep your paws off that bush-girl,' his mother groaned
from her bed. 'I've been watching. So soon as you throw them over
they put a spell on you. I know them.'

When Tant' Philipa died there was no excuse for having the girl
around, so she had to return to the location for good.

'You know of the ghost in the Kloof?' he had asked her once in
the out-house.

'Ghost? Ach, it's but old spook stories,' she had giggled. 'You
afraid of spooks then?'

'You people don't mos go near there.'

'*Bygelofies*,' the girl said. 'Superstitions. For a white man you
are very superstitious.'

'Boss,' he said, frowning. 'You call me boss. And my ma knows
about such things.'

He felt a little irked that the girl had dared contradict him. But if
she did not believe such things, perhaps there was nothing to it
after all. He did not bother too much about such matters again. The
girl did not prove a witch, there was lots to do about the farm, and
Meulen was having a new house built.

Then there was the time of the jongnoi Meulen's wedding and
those two drunken blacks running amok. Who would have thought
one of them would have died, tied up like that to the fence post all
night? And then the other had cut his arm open when he and
Hannes Meulen had gone to release them the next morning. Well,
the one kaffir was dead, that was not to be helped, but the judge
had been rather hard on the boss over it. And it served that other
black right when he was sent to prison for attempting to murder
him, Jaap Opperman. There he was with twelve stitches and his
arm in a sling for weeks, not being able to do his work well, and the
blerry blacks looking sullen.

But they *had* tied those two blacks up out in the open on a
bitterly cold night and one of them had died. He hadn't *meant* for
the stupid bogger to go and die. He remembered his mother, with
her herbs and roots and black superstitions, saying: 'You treat
them strict but right. You never know what hex they can put on
you.'

Well, no black bogger was going to put the hex on *him*. Spooks.
Bloody spook stories. But he did not like the sullen way the other
farm labourers looked at him. He was in charge and they had to

jump when the boss spoke.

'A black knows snakes,' his mother said. The blerry truth. Here had been a verdomde black snake bit him in the arm, so to speak. Only he had used a broken bottle.

When he could use his arm again he decided to go across and look at that cursed and tantalising Kloof once and for all. He didn't tell anybody — there would be too much superstitious *rumoer*. It was going to be a hot day and he donned an old felt hat, khaki shorts and velskoens and set out across the blooming grassland.

The Kloof was a long way off of course, anybody knew that. So he had also brought a packet of sandwiches and a water canteen. Spring covered the land, and the veld blossoms were out all over.

He reached the low brown foothills, and towards midday was scouting around under the flat and blue-white sky until he found a rough track, ocre sand and pebbles, that led to the mouth of the ravine. It had the appearance of any other small ravine and he wondered again what all the fuss was about.

A lone *aasvogel* circled lazily overhead for a while and then went away.

The mouth of the cut was overgrown with wild purple heather, some spiny plants and cactus sprouting from among the rocks and fallen stones. The walls of the cut were neither steep, abrupt, nor in any way frightening. A long-tailed bird darted out from among some bushes and ground-hopped like a low-flying airplane. Jaap thrust aside the undergrowth and trod pebbles up the ravine. There was no sign of ancient burial, unless an untidy pile of stones on a flat table was a grave. Otherwise the place was just a cleft strewn with boulders and rockfall, grown with patches of underbrush, thorns and desert flowers.

He thought, so much for the ghost of the black chief.

He wiped moisture from his brow and took a drink from his canteen. Then he went a little further up the Kloof, looking about. He thought: I should have brought a witness, to prove to everybody.

Further along the Kloof his step dislodged a loose stone and he heard the dangerous hissing as the common and venom-laden old *ringhals* which had been asleep there woke up and struck swiftly at his bare leg.

★

Only those who were awake with the dawn saw the colour of it in the sky. The sky was a great round bowl, so that for a moment those who saw it felt as though they were above, looking down into it. Then sky and land brimmed with a rosy flood of light that rolled westward to check and break and foam against the low hills and the broken crags, and the land filled with the powdered haze of yet another hot day.

When Edgar Stopes woke up in the little room the sun was already making barred patterns across the drab walls, the wardrobe, the faded picture of aloes, and he lay stickily in the narrow iron cot. Sounds from the lower part of the hotel vaguely touched his mind. He had drunk the half jack of brandy, on top of the beer, and his brain felt as ponderous as a bolt of flannel. A bird screamed somewhere, jarring his nerves like the edge of a rasp, but it was not a bird, and he remembered painfully that Mrs Kroner had said early breakfast this morning because of the church service.

He lay prone and sweatily in the bed and thought — them, let them shove the breakfast where the monkey puts his nuts. Anyway, he was in no shape for breakfast. He recailed all the cheap hotels, the innumerable plates of cornflakes, the greasy bacon and over-fried eggs like scorched plastic. What he needed was a *babalas* drink, something to pull him straight, to get him ticking again, but of course the bloody pub downstairs would be shut. He lay there in the ill-featured room like a prisoner held in by bars of yellow sunlight, feeling the bolt of flannel unroll itself with aching slowness. Mrs Kroner shouted again, something about mealie-casserole for midday, and to cap it all the bell of the church across the square began to toll.

The iron sound of the bell in the tower sent the birds flapping nervously from the roof of the church, their cries harsh as they made wildly for the eaves of the row of shops in the square. The square and the front street were beginning to fill with pick-up trucks, dusty cars and Cape-carts, wagons and Land Rovers. Under the trees the farm trucks donated towards the removal of the blacks were parked. The Police Sergeant had left his constable in charge of the station while he too attended church before accompanying the trucks. It was expected that all the local dignitaries join in the prayers for rain.

The square crunched with the sound of shoes on gravel as the townsfolk and those who had come in from the outlying farms made their way towards the area below the wide doorway at the top of the red concrete steps.

The women had had their Sunday dresses ironed and the children's kisklere had been taken out of camphor. Old mothers in cloche hats of decades ago hooked the arms of their men who had put on their best suits, perspiring in navy serge and funeral black, doffing their broad-banded, stiff, felt hats to neighbours. Butterfly collars and black ties strained around ruddy necks. They were the elders, the younger set had come in their best lounge suits, looking a little awkward in the presence of dark formality. Others had donned their wedding outfits, preserved for occasions such as this. The young women, somehow both cool and sunburnt, looked demure in sunhats and print dresses, while the scrubbed children itched and fretted in thick cloth and uncomfortable shoes.

Those who had not met recently stopped in the square outside the church to exchange greetings, pleasantries, information, gossip, advice. The townswomen invited those from outside to coffee and rusks after the service, and all shrilled at the children playing around the Boer War monument. The men shook hands, thick, stubby hands, pink smoothness cracked across with chalky white wrinkles.

'*More*, Oom; morning, Tante.'

'Ai, is the weather not *verskriklik?* It's all I can do to keep the plants alive.'

'*Wragtig*. Piet is trying to keep the pump going — the poor sheep.'

'Ja, it will affect the prices, I tell you.'

'Morning, Hannes, how is the campaign going?'

'Oh, there is nothing to it. The voting will be a mere formality.'

'How are you, Rina? *Magtig*, you are looking pretty. Hannes, it's a pity your Pa can't come.'

'Ja, but he's much too old. Perhaps I'll ask the Dominee to come out with me.'

Rina hung upon Meulen's arm, blushing as compliments were bestowed on her. She was the future wife of the future member of the Volksraad. They stood in the centre of a lapping pool of admirers and smiled and nodded and shook hands.

The Police Sergeant came up, thick and heavy as a load of sand, yet spruce and at ease in his uniform — he did not have to change into strange and unusual clothes very often. 'Meneer Meulen, I see your trucks are here. Thank you, hey.'

'Do you have enough transport?'

'Enough for the purpose, ja. Those kaffirs don't have much belongings.'

'Bantu,' Kasper Steen corrected. 'They are called Bantu.'

The Sergeant looked at him. 'Bantu. Quite right. Bantu, meneer.'

The Bantu Commissioner who had joined them, said: 'Do you know what they got up to? They actually sent two loafers to see me again yesterday. Something about having deep roots. Deep roots, I ask you!'

'What did they mean?'

'The Almighty alone knows.'

'Will they make trouble?' Steen asked.

The Sergeant said, 'Don't trouble yourselves, your honours. Everything is in hand. What can those *skepsels* do? A few old men and women. Leave everything to me. They respect the law.'

'Yes, I suppose so,' the Commissioner agreed. 'One must depend on the law.'

The church bell was still tolling and the deacon had opened the doors, the congregation making its way slowly up the steps, relieved to get out of the morning heat, mopping the perspiration from noses and necks as the sun blazed down on their dark clothes. In the wilting greenery insects buzzed with drowsy unconcern.

Inside the church there was an immense hush. Thick carpeting deadened the sound of feet as the worshippers dispersed into the pews. It was still run in the old style, women separated from their men, and the front pews paid for by the important families. An austere yet expensive church, all polished stinkwood, teak and imbuia, and tall windows; with oak and pine for the lesser folk. The organ, when the service opened, boomed and trumpeted like the hosts of Heaven, while the Dominee in gown of mourning black with double row of black tassels, ascended into the pulpit like a dark messenger come to announce the death of God. The birds across the square rose again from their perches to make off across the scorched fields.

The opening hymn gasped shakily to an end, drowned in the torrent of organ music. The Dominee waited for the shuffling to die away, his slightly protuberant, pale and Teutonic eyes surveying the conglomeration of faces below. He knew that he received the deepest veneration for each of his syllables, that in the community structure his status was godlike, and that his sonorous voice was that of God speaking through him was undisputed. The hush lay again over the congregation, punctuated here and there by a suppressed cough. Beyond the windows the heat lay cadmium yellow on the street:

Oh kings of Judah. and inhabitants of Jerusalem . . . Behold, I will bring evil upon this place, the which whosoever heareth, his ears shall tingle. Because they have forsaken me, and have estranged this place, and have burned incense in it unto other gods whom neither they nor their fathers have known, nor the kings of Judah, and have filled this place with the blood of innocents; They have built also the high places of Baal, . . . which I commanded not, nor spake it, neither came it into my mind: Therefore, behold, the days come . . . that this place shall no more be called Tophet, nor The valley of the son of Hinnom, but The valley of slaughter.

Having read, the Dominee Visser looked up from the Book, peering over his pince-nez, removed them and squeezed the pulpit rails with his thick hands as if to milk them of spiritual support.

'My children, you all know why we have gathered here in this holy place this special morning. For months now the Living Lord has seen fit to withhold from this land the precious rain on which we depend for the flourishing of our food, our life. He has taken from us the life-giving waters. The land starves and thirsts and the livestock die. Why? we ask. Why? Tell us, O Lord, we pray.

Oh kings of Judah, and inhabitants of Jerusalem . . . Behold, I will bring evil upon this place, the which whosoever heareth, his ears shall tingle. . . .

So did God speak to Jeremiah and so does he speak to us.

'For we have turned from the Lord. *Baldness is come upon Gaza; Ashkelon is cut off with the remnant of their valley: how long wilt thou cut thyself?*

'But what sin have we committed? we ask ourselves. Do we not walk daily in the path of the Lord? Can I point at you and say, You and you have committed such and such a sin? My children, we each of us go through life trying to commit no sin and believe that is enough. But have we looked about us? We the inhabitants of Jerusalem, for is not all our beloved land Jerusalem?

'There is corruption in our cities. The courts are inundated with cases of crime and lechery. Only recently there was tried in the court in one of our cities an affair concerning an exhibition of lewd

105

and lustful so-called art pictures; in a club open to our youth and womenfolk there was given a performance by a woman — can she be called a woman? — dancing near-naked with a snake, the symbol of evil. I was appalled to read of the incidences of suicide among what we call teenagers — fifty-five thousand over the last fifteen years. There is the taking of hallucinatory drugs among certain young people. Many of our young women deliberately defile their purity by wearing revealing clothes.

'Are these manifestations of our true way of life? Of our civilisation? Can we wonder that the Lord God withholds His bounty from this land? Is this the example which we set our wards, those whom God gave into our care to be guided along His path?

'*Woe unto Nebo! for it is spoiled*: Can you go complacently through life and say, This has nothing to do with me. I did not do it? Are we here not affected by the sins of others? Am I not my brother's keeper?'

The priest's hands drummed the pulpit as if sending out a message which his voice only echoed. 'Again, are the sins of the fathers not visited upon the children? The decline of civilisations, the disappearance of a way of life, does not only come through defeat in war or superiority in victory. The heathen around us have blighted us since the times of our forefathers who delivered this country into our hands. The victors sinned against keeping the blood pure. Sin came with the mixing of blood as sure as Adam ate of the forbidden apple. Blood pollution and the lowering of the racial level which goes with it, are the only cause why old civilisations disappear. The causes are not lost wars, but the lost power of resistance which ensures the purity of the blood. See what is happening to the Portuguese civilisation in the north. How has integration and assimilation helped them?

'In the purity of our blood also lies the guarantee of our honourable mission. It is the duty of all of us to unshakeably keep to our aim, spiritual and earthly, which is to secure for our children their God-given land and soil on this earth. Holding to this aim is the only means of acquiring forgiveness of sins of the past, of purifying the blood again, in the name of God and our nation. Just as our forefathers had to do battle against the heathen for their lives and for the soil on which we live today, so also now and in the future, life will not grant to our people new soil as a favour, but only as it is won through the power of the victorious word of God.'

Dominee Visser paused, realising that somewhere or other along the way he must have lost the thread of his discourse. But he felt there was no need for logic for he could see his audience hanging rapt to his words. They were fundamentally a simple people and took what he said for granted.

'It is not enough to come here to pray for the Lord's goodness and bounty. His rewards go to the deserving. The heathen beats his spears against our door. The Philistines are returning once more with their awful gods and terrible sacrifices. They are breaking into our civilisation, into the minds of civilised people, civilisation is threatened. It is our ignorance of this that has caused God to send drought as a reminder that He lives, that He has been forgotten. God is just, and punishes us for our laxity.

And joy and gladness is taken from the plentiful field, and from the land of Moab; and I have caused wine to fail from the winepresses; none shall tread with shouting; their shouting shall be no shouting.

'Therefore I say to you, my children, rise up out of your sloth and your ignorance. Take up again the sword of your forefathers so that the land may be protected from the heathen and made safe for God and our nation. Then only shall the Lord make the soil bountiful. Now let us pray for His mercy and forgiveness.'

In the square the farm-trucks made a clamour as the drivers gunned the engines. The Sergeant of Police was in his armoured Land Rover with the clerk from the Bantu Commissioner's office. On the steps of the church the Dominee was shaking hands with members of the congregation as they came out into the quivering sunlight, and some of them watched the trucks moving out from under the trees.

An elderly man with flaky red skin was shaking hands with Hannes Meulen and saying, 'It was a fine sermon the Dominee gave. A warning. As for me, I would rather be accused a thousand times of being a racist than of being a traitor to the cause of the white man.'

He lifted his hat to Rina Steen who smiled gaily at him, saying, '*Totsiens*, Oom.' The elderly man went across the square, walking carefully, feeling his way with a mahogany stick, and Rina, fanning herself with a handkerchief, said to Meulen: 'You mustn't forget to come and have midday meal with us, liefling.'

Crossing the square the trucks turned into the front street and went out of the little town, the red dust boiling behind them and settling on the plate-glass, the doors and the walls of the houses and locked stores.

★

From the street came the sounds of motor engines being started up, gears changing, the noise of traffic leaving the little dorp as people headed back to the farms. Others would stay on a little longer, go visiting, gossip over *melktert* on the stoeps, or talk over the Dominee's sermon, the weather, creaking in their best clothes, fanning moist faces with newly-ironed handkerchiefs. Relenting parents would allow the children to take off the uncomfortable shoes so they could wiggle their toes in the hot dust of the garden lots. On the whole it would be a visiting day: the special service for rain had provided fringe benefits. But those who ran the town's business had to resume their functions at the little cafes, the garage, the grocers, the offices of the local authorities, the grain store.

Voices in the street came to him like the sounds made by distant birds as Edgar Stopes sat on the unmade bed and told himself that as soon as the shops and stores opened he would be setting about taking their orders. He hoped the mechanic would have got his car in running order by the time he had done the rounds of the town. He would have to stretch out time, buttering up the shopkeepers, talking about the drought, business, the health of the womenfolk, the saving to be made on the bulk purchase of tea-strainers.

You're stuck with it he thought. Failure and hopelessness clung to him like hairspray — the new-style aerosol cans of failure at thirty-five cents each wholesale. Sold over the counter you made a profit in failure. Hopelessness hung on the stained walls of hotel rooms, with the prints of aloes in bloom, the calendar girls, the wardrobes that had to be propped closed. Hopelessness and failure were double images peering at one from cracked mirrors over dusty dressing-tables; tickled at sweaty skin in the beds made up with sheets frayed by bitterness and darned with despair.

The molten-gold sunlight glared on the withered and scorched garden below the window and he sat, stubbly and grimy, in the roomful of stale and warm shade with the railway picture and his suitcase crammed with soiled washing and the spring-back binders of catalogued egg-beaters and alarm clocks.

But the old go-getting spirit stirred somewhere inside him again, something exposed under the disturbed scum of stagnant water, and he thought, his moustache twitching, well, *en avant*, march, old pal, the rolling stone gathers no moss; there's suckers out there just waiting to be sold loads of clothes-pegs. He chuckled sourly and said aloud: 'Dammit, it's still me here, hey, good ol' Edgar Stopes.' He pulled on his dressing-gown, found his shaving kit, and went out to the bathroom.

Later, shaved and smelling of lotion, he came out of the room, his suit straightened, catalogue and orderbook under an arm. Downstairs, kitchenware clanged and Mrs Kroner screamed, 'Wonderful sermon. Where's that *vervloekte* Fanie again?' His head still throbbed, but he was full of bitter cheer again. 'Blast them all, the long and the short and the tall,' he sang under his breath, and there was this tall and handsome Dutch joker coming out of another room into the hallway, locking it and saying, 'Ah, good morning, meneer.'

'Hullo, Mister Dingus,' Edgar Stopes smiled. Good fellowship rose in him, bright and unstable as a bunch of coloured balloons. 'How are you then? A good service, I hear.'

'Oh, the reverend spoke well,' Hannes Meulen replied. 'On your rounds?'

Edgar Stopes tapped the catalogue and order-book. 'The shops ought to be opening now. Must keep the folks supplied, hey? Mustn't let them run short.' He laughed. 'Staying to sample our dear Missus Kroner's mealie-cheese, dingus?'

Meulen returned the laugh, showing his fine white teeth and Edgar Stopes thought of artificial pearl bracelets, very nice with your evening-wear. 'No, I'm lunching out, man. Mealie-cheese. Anyway, I am leaving here today.'

'Can't see a person like you in an hotel like this.'

'Oh, Missus Kroner does her best.'

They reached the head of the stairs and Edgar Stopes bowed with mock gallantry, ushering Meulen forward. 'Honour before beauty, old cock,' he joked, but his mind sang, blast them all, the long and the short and the tall. He thought, fingering his moustache, bladdy Member of Parliament my bladdy eye. What's he got that a bloke like me haven't?

Meulen said, 'I suppose that you will come this way again? Know everybody in town, neh?'

'Only the business people really,' Stopes said, following the other man down. 'I reckon a man can get to know a place by the local business. You can judge if a place is getting on or not by the total of orders placed. Now take a little place like this for example ...'

At the foot of the staircase they edged around each other in the narrow passageway and Meulen smiled again, saying, 'Well, I must be off now, sir. I take the short cut by the back way.'

Edgar Stopes thought okey, high and bloody mightiness, if you can't stand a bit of decent conversation, but said instead, 'Everything of the best then.' In the kitchen nearby, Mrs Kroner was saying, 'Did you peel the potatoes?'

Beyond Hannes Meulen, at the end of the short corridor, the open back door framed a rectangle of gaudy sunlight and a growth of wilting shrubbery in the thirsting garden, and glancing past Meulen as the latter turned towards it, Edgar Stopes saw the sunlight irregularly obscured by the face and form of the black man who Meulen also saw but did not recognise.

Hannes Meulen did not recognise his own latest model automatic shotgun either, but wondered for a second why the black man had it because that wasn't allowed; behind him Edgar Stopes saw the look of anger, then the flash and heard the blast, and the next thing there was a slither and a heavy thump together with a wet slap across his cheek which was made by one of Hannes Meulen's ears as his head was blown off, and the whitewash of the passage-wall was suddenly decorated with a blossom petalled with blood and brains and pieces of bone and fragments of teeth like pomegranate pips.

Edgar Stopes, still holding his catalogue and order-book, knowing something was wrong, stared open-mouthed back at the single eye of the shotgun that was leaking foul-smelling vapour, and somewhere he could hear a nerve-tormenting, birdlike shrieking while his bowels turned helpless and his mind cried out to somebody called Maisie, but the sound of the tortured bird was the only sound he heard as the next blast killed him.

*

The Sergeant led the little convoy of farm lorries across the countryside, their wheels grinding the dry and brittle sand of the road, sending it clicking against metalwork and windscreens. On the side of the sand road, across the fields thorn trees rose like gnarled hands. In front of the untidy horizon the heat, dressed in stripes of hazy blue, danced a jig. The convoy lurched drunkenly on along the crumbling bank of the stream bed until it had to stop before reaching the first houses of the village because its right of way was obstructed by felled bluegum trees thrown across the sunken track.

Beyond this barricade the Sergeant could see a few old people, crones and hunched men like crude carvings, sitting in the doorways of earthen-walled houses; but it was the crowd gathering in the dusty space under some standing trees, having heard the trucks, that held his attention. He had a feeling that things were not as they should be.

'Come on,' he said to the Bantu Commissioner's clerk, and climbed down from the Land Rover. The clerk, who had changed from his church clothes to sports shirt and khaki shorts, looked a little apprehensively at the Sergeant and then climbed out on the other side of the vehicle, carrying a file of official papers.

At the sight of these two the crowd in the patch of ground under the trees commenced to sing. This irked the Sergeant. He did not care for blacks singing. When blacks started to sing, there was almost always trouble. He marched heavily towards the barricade of trees, his dewdrop eyes angry in their loose, discoloured pouches of flesh not unlike used tea-bags, calling: 'What is all this, hey?'

Somebody, a hefty woman in rough clothes and a leather belt, whom he recognised as the headman's sister, waved thick black arms and the crowd quietened. The woman's voice boomed across to him: 'It is not necessary to come further.'

The Sergeant stopped short of the barricade. He had not meant to do so and thought that this was a mistake; one had to exert authority at all times. To make up for this, he refused to acknowledge the woman and asked, 'Who are you? No, I don't want to talk to you. Where is Hlangeni? Don't you people know you must move today? And what are these trees doing here? Look, we have even brought the lorries.'

'The lorries are useless,' the woman said across the space between them. 'We are not going to move. Your magistrate was told this.'

'I don't want to talk to you,' the Sergeant said coldly. 'Where is the headman, Hlangeni?' He addressed the crowd. 'Do not listen to this woman. She is only here for trouble, I know.'

A man who he knew as Kobe or something like that, said: 'There is no Hlangeni. Hlangeni is not of these people.'

There was a general murmur and the crowd shuffled and then the singing broke out again.

The Sergeant took a step forward. 'What is going on?' he shouted. 'You know that today you must trek.' He gestured at the clerk with the file of papers. 'Here is the boss with the orders from the government. The same papers that were handed to Hlangeni.'

Kobe looked at the clerk and said, 'He is only a boy.'

The Sergeant said sharply, 'You have to have some respect for the government. Don't be a fool. Tell your people to bring their stuff to the lorries.'

Now the woman laughed a booming laugh. 'There is too much talking. It is time you left here yourself.'

Then the people commenced to sing again, moving with the rhythm of the song. The Sergeant lost his temper and started to unbutton his pistol holster. There was a cry mingling with the song, a sort of ululation from the women, and a youth hurled a stone at the Sergeant. It missed him, but the clerk panicked and fled, dropping his file of papers, the official documents skidding across the sand. The Sergeant had his revolver out and fired into the air, but the stones came thick now. The clerk was climbing wildly into the Land Rover as a rock bounced from the wire mesh over the windscreen. Along the little convoy the drivers were frantically starting the lorries, grinding and clashing the gears as the chanting crowd of villagers advanced behind the hail of stones that starred windows and gashed paintwork.

The Police Sergeant holstered his revolver and turned to lumber red-faced towards his Land Rover, realising that he could not handle this alone, that he would have to send for reinforcements. Who would have thought that these bloody kaffirs would start something like this? He had been defeated by a lot of baboons in jumble-sale clothing. What was everything coming to?

A stone knocked his uniform hat off and it rolled in the dust with the clerk's official papers. He reached the Land Rover and climbed heavily in behind the armour. The stones kept coming across the barricade of trees and clanged on the metal of the trucks as they churned the dust, manoeuvring to turn about and head back down the road. Behind them the crowd were singing their outlandish song.

★

The Coca Cola went flat in the glass, but Maisie did not bother, thinking that doing something like *that* was all right on the films, but when it came to the real thing, why, it was sort of cruel.

Around her the cutlery tinkled in the first-floor cafeteria, and she sat among the debris of late breakfasts: spilled tea, paper cups, half-eaten éclairs and toasted cheese, while the Muzak quietly played pop music behind the whispers from the short sleeves, cropped heads, the aroma of deodorant. Somebody said, '. . . but I gave her a piece of my mind, hey.' The bloody kaffir girl had not turned up that morning and so Maisie had not had breakfast in bed. 'It's getting too much of a good thing,' Mrs Muller next door had complained.

Opposite the cafeteria a wall advertised air trips to Europe; and in the distance beyond the end of the street, beyond the traffic lights at the intersection, the stolid and ugly drum design of the Ponte building disturbed the sky that already shook with heat. Somewhere, unsynchronised, church bells made a faraway jangle. The cafeteria was on the first floor of a department store that landmarked the end of that part of the old section: you could see the railway bridge and a section of wire fence, the tops of billboards.

God, you can't just think like that. They hang you for murder — even women. Like Mrs Lee. Well, she was not going to be saddled with that Wally Basson any longer, not that way. It had been all right while it lasted, she supposed. She hadn't had a time like that with Edgar. So where will you go, what will you do? So what *about* the army? The country is in danger, join up, she thought theatrically, and laughed at herself. Not on your bloody life, old girl. Oh, damn, if only Edgar would sort of die from, well, *natural* causes.

Around her isolated groups and couples in summer clothes drank iced squash. The heat throbbed outside the balcony, and even in here liquid absorbed through mouths was quickly shed by the skin. Out of sight, at the end of the street, above the falsetto of traffic there was a sound of singing, like a choir chanting in the distance.

Well, he *is* worth two thousand pounds, that poor, loud-mouthed, big-talker. Looking up absently, she saw her face distorted in plate-glass, the green eyes two pairs of faulty glass marbles, the pink rouged mouth suddenly joined by another. Two doll-faces gazed bitterly back at her, merging with the backs of heads in the cubicle on the other side of the glass.

A group of policemen in dark and pale blue went in a straggling file up the street, past the store front and towards the intersection, moving at a lope. Far up the street from the intersection, the traffic seemed to have piled up and there was a blur of close-packed human heads.

Maisie thought, so you're stuck with Edgar, that's all. For a time, anyway; she amended optimistically. Something will come up. She sipped the Coke absently and remembered a country club, gins and lime, a band playing under gaudy lights. Some of the customers in the cafeteria got up from their tables, leaving carrier bags to go to the edge of the balcony. A voice said, 'Must be this day of prayer business, a procession.'

A traffic policeman in crash helmet and white half-sleeves was holding up the normal traffic for a truck-load of police in green and khaki camouflage and jungle hats. The truck edged by the traffic and parked, and the men in their baggy, splotched gear climbed down carrying automatic rifles. Another similar cargo of police troops came up, together with a Land Rover enclosed with wire mesh containing a trainer with several Alsatian hounds.

Up the street where the traffic was stalled, the mass of heads drew into focus and the singing took form.

From the balcony those who looked down saw another mass of singing people, men and women, advancing down this street towards the crossing. The column of black people were singing together, a marching song.

At the crossing an officer of police was diverting some constables and paramilitary police to block off the second column of marchers. There were armed men in helmets, some carrying long riot staves.

The manager of the cafeteria came out, calling: 'Ladies and gentlemen, please come off this balcony now. There might be an er- accident.'

'Not on your life,' somebody laughed. 'We want to see the fun.'

There was a crowd at the balustrade now, all looking down. Maisie found herself involuntarily wedged in by talcum powder and after-shave, and she thought, I don't want anything to do with this. She said, 'Excuse me, please,' trying to get away from the press.

A voice said, 'Day of prayer, bloody hell, hey. The damn nignogs are on the rampage.'

'Maybe they're only going to the services.'

'Oh, the police will handle the buggers.'

'Well. we do pay taxes.'

The manager appealed: 'Ladies and gentlemen, you must come

inside, please.' He repeated this in Afrikaans to make it official, it seemed.

The column of marchers passed the cafeteria, below the balcony, led by a man with a flag. At the end of the street, at the traffic lights, a line of green-and-khaki was drawn up. In the middle of the crossing another crowd was already clashing with the police, exploding in a spray of humanity and snarling dogs, swinging staves. Onlookers were fleeing up the sidewalks away from the scene.

The manager made another desperate appeal: 'The management will not hold itself responsible for any injuries sustained.' It was as if he was reading off an official notice at the end of a railway platform. While he was making this announcement, the men in khaki-and-green fired off several canisters of tear-gas at the demonstrators below. The canisters bounced in the street and shed their white, cottony fumes. A section of riot police, grotesque in masks, charged the crowd, swinging their long staves.

'There, you see,' the manager cried above the Muzak and the sound of battle.

Maisie was dragging herself away. She saw through a triangle made by a sunburnt and peeling elbow that the crowd of blacks had broken, some running back and others defiantly closing with the police in the gas that hung foggily in the street. A window broke with the sound of falling bells. Police sirens bayed in the distance. In the gutter and on the sidewalk lay bundles of clothes that sprouted feet, hands, and faces like red-painted masks. Maisie was momentarily reminded of Guy Fawkes night when she was a child. A woman went up the street holding her bleeding face, and Maisie, extricating herself, thought illogically, Poor old Edgar, I reckon I'm stuck with him. Pity stirred in her, an alien worm, and she resigned herself, with a last glimpse of a huddled mound, I reckon I'm stuck with him.

People on the balcony were coughing and the manager was repeating anxiously, 'You see, I told you we cannot be held responsible.'

At the end of the street, by the railway bridge, the swirl of black people rallied and advanced again. The police in uniform and camouflage clothes fired off another volley of tear-gas and then moved to meet the crowd.

*

Long ago the wind and rain and trickling rivulets had cut the surface of the earth with a network of gullies, narrow here, wide and deep there, like exposed veins. Around the edges of the dongas the parched fields quivered in the haze, and in the foothills where the deep cuts started the land was rough and stony. One could see where the Kloof opened, a dry wound in the earth that was held in mysterious respect by folk; it was difficult to say why. There were many stories about it. First there was one story, told generations in the past, then people added to this story or made up others so that the original was lost, a pebble dropped among others, covered by layers of sand blown by the wind. It was not really known why this particular cut in the hills had been chosen for legend and tales; it was a gap in the hills like so many others. But there it was, and nobody went there any more.

Madonele the shepherd, driving the meagre herd up the sandy stream bed in the foothills, saw the mouth of the Kloof some way to the side, and this made him want to compose a story in his mind. He flicked his switch at the dusty sheep on the edge of the herd. At the tail end loped the old hound, cutting off any stragglers. They were a long way from the village having started out early that morning, following the twists and turns of the scarred countryside. He couldn't find a story being too concerned about what was to take place, so he tucked the seed of an idea away in the folds of his mind until such time as he was able to sit quietly by the fire of contemplation.

The little hooves of the sheep churned the sand. Here and there red dust rose in tiny clouds. This was a region of dry and dusty stretches of reddish-yellow land made harsh by the drought. It was a land of ridges and low, rocky koppies and withered thorn trees, of sandstone and basalt. Here a table of reddish sandstone hid the hills; there a tall wedge of strata stood like a gigantic slice of petrified layer cake. The scattered karoo bush mottled the surface of the soil.

The shepherd knew where there was shade and the remains of a pool. By scratching away the surface crust and digging, it was possible to reach wet mud and water below. The hollow in the ground accounted for the water collecting during the wet season. The rains soaked through the sand, through the gravel beneath and gathered in a basin of clay below.

Madonele was thinking about this when he saw the man sitting in the sketchy shade of a stunted tree at the side of the stream bed.

'You and your sheep,' the man said with mock derision. He sat with his back against the rough trunk, his knees drawn up. There were patches of sweat staining his shirt and he looked as if he had been walking hard before stopping to rest. He had taken off his boots and they stood beside him while he dug his toes in the dust.

Madonele the shepherd whistled and signalled the old hound to rest the little herd between the crumbling banks. He trudged through the dust towards the man, his eyes bright under the tattered hat, flicking his branchwood switch.

'So it is you,' he said and squatted on his haunches near the man. He shook his head and with a finger like a twig, wiped dust from the sockets of his little brown eyes. 'You came far and even ahead of me.'

'I'm not slowed down by sheep,' the man called Shilling Murile replied. 'And I walked straight across country.'

'You know the country from the old days.'

'Why not? One remembers.'

The shepherd reached under his thin and tattered blanket and produced a bottle filled with water. It had a loop of twine at the neck for carrying. He worked the cork out slowly and held the bottle towards Shilling Murile. 'Wet your throat. It is very dry work, walking all that distance.'

The other smiled primly and said, 'After you, old one.'

'How respectful.'

The shepherd tilted the bottle and sucked water, belched and said, 'I am glad that you are safe.'

'Safe?' Murile took the bottle and after two gulps handed it back, rolled the water in his mouth and then swallowed. 'Who is safe?'

The shepherd replaced the cork and asked, his eyes lowered: 'Tell me, did you do what you came to do?'

'I do not wish to talk about such things now. Say that my brother Timi rests peacefully.'

An ant came out of its hole and trundled across a stretch of sand. It was merely a patch, but to the ant it probably seemed an expanse of desert.

'They will come after you.'

'How? Do they know me?'

'Hmmm! Then you must join with us, the villagers, and be lost among us. But they will be coming after the villagers too. The woman said they would send police and even flying machines.'

117

The ant circled a blade of cracked grass and went out of sight down a crease in the sand.

'Where are they now, the village people?'

'Mma-Tau brings them into the hills.'

'They will not stay long and the police will round everybody up,' Shilling Murile said. 'It will only be a showing.'

'They will have showed their unwillingness to be enslaved,' the shepherd said. He frowned and the wizened face looked sullen under the ragged hat. 'It is our land after all,' he said.

'And I will be bullied by that woman,' the one called Shilling Murile said. Then he reached aside and brought out from under his blouse the new automatic shotgun which had belonged to Hannes Meulen. 'And this?' he asked.

Madonele looked at the weapon that shone in the sunlight. He said, 'Hauw!' His voice was awed and he reached out gingerly with a dusty finger. 'May one touch it?' He jerked the finger back as the hot metal burned him, and sucked it. 'Will you keep it?'

Murile had put the weapon down on his jacket again, and was pulling on his boots. He shrugged, 'Why not? We might find out what can be done with it. I have a few shells left for it.'

'Let us keep it then,' Madonele said. He added, peering at the other. 'You said *we*. Are you coming with our people?'

Shilling Murile got up, holding the shotgun wrapped in his blouse. He looked at the shepherd and his broad perspiring face moved slightly in a smile. 'Let us say that I am coming with *you*, old man,' he said. 'Remember, you have my tobacco.'

Madonele the shepherd tittered and turned away, whistled to the hound, and the sheep commenced to move through the dust. Shilling Murile slid down the bank, the loose earth giving under his weight, and plodded after the shepherd, his boots crunching the dry soil.

★

The hard sun beats fully down and whenever something moves the dust whips up like fire smoke. Everywhere the land stands against a dazzling light. In the distance, behind a blue haze, lies the faint suggestion of mountains. The sun, a smear of bronze, turns the light of the world a cruel metallic yellow in the furnace-hot time of the day. Now there is a harshness and a hardness in the land that foretells little sympathy for the weak. The drought-ridden floor of the country projects its white glitter that stretches away until lost in the smoky haze while the torturing sun blazes on.

It seems that the air, heavy with heat, begins to move. It has weight; it moves soundlessly and heavily, gathering momentum. The blanket of heat yields to great pressures. Something has created a movement of the hotter air that must find its way upward, to give place to cooler air that must find its way down. The wind signals its rising with a low moan which precedes many others. The movement of the wind builds up and carries the stinging dust; the veils of dust cross the land like the smoke from lines of artillery and the moaning of the wind rises to a roar that is the sound of a blast furnace carrying a myriad needles of fire. The land bends and sags under the power of the moving heat. Then the thrust of the wind lessens and the difference in air makes life possible again. The roaring dies away.

The yellowing afternoon light puts a golden colour on the land. A flight of birds swoop overhead towards a water-hole.

THE AFRICAN WRITERS SERIES

The book you have been reading is part of Heinemann's long-established series of African fiction. A list of the other titles available in this series is given below, but for a catalogue giving information on all the titles available in this series and in the Caribbean Writers series write to:

Heinemann Educational Publishers,
Halley Court, Jordan Hill, Oxford OX2 8EJ
or e-mail: export.repp@repp.co.uk

United States customers should write to Heinemann Inc,
361 Hanover Street, Portsmouth NH 03801-3959
or e-mail: custserv@heinemann.com

The Sun Hath Looked Upon Me, Calixthe Beyala
Your Name Shall Be Tanga, Calixthe Beyala
I Write What I Like, Steve Biko (not available in the USA)
A Duty of Memory, WPB Botha
Wantok, WPB Botha
The Heinemann Book of African Women's Writing, Charlotte Bruner (ed)
Unwinding Threads, Charlotte Bruner (ed)
Harvest of Thorns, Shimmer Chinodya
(available in Zimbabwe through Baobab Books)
Every Man Is A Race, Mia Couto
Voices Made Night, Mia Couto
Beyond the Horizon, Amma Darko
The Housemaid, Amma Darko
The Marabi Dance, Modikwe Dikobe
The Strange Man, Amu Djoleto
Burning Grass, Cyprian Ekwensi
Jagua Nana, Cyprian Ekwensi
The Bride Price, Buchi Emecheta (not available in the USA or Canada)
Head Above Water, Buchi Emecheta
In The Ditch, Buchi Emecheta
The Joys of Motherhood, Buchi Emecheta
Kehinde, Buchi Emecheta
Second Class Citizen, Buchi Emecheta (not available in the USA or Canada)
The Slave Girl, Buchi Emecheta (not available in the USA or Canada)
Equiano's Travels, Olaudah Equiano, Paul Edwards (ed)
Crimes of Conscience, Nadine Gordimer (not available in Canada)
The Cardinals, Bessie Head (not available in South Africa)
The Collector of Treasures, Bessie Head
Maru, Bessie Head
A Question of Power, Bessie Head
Tales of Tenderness and Power, Bessie Head (not available in South Africa)
When Rain Clouds Gather, Bessie Head
A Woman Alone: Autobiographical Writings, Bessie Head
The Heinemann Book of South African Short Stories,
Denis Hirson with Martin Trump (eds)
We Killed Mangy-Dog and Other Stories, Louis Bernardo Honwana
Eyes of the Sky, Rayda Jacobs (not available in South Africa)
The Enemy Within, Steve Jacobs
Ambiguous Adventure, Cheikh Hamidou Kane
(not available in the USA or Canada)
Kicking Tongues, Karen King-Aribisala
The Clothes of Nakedness, Benjamin Kwame Kwakye
A Walk in the Night, Alex La Guma
In the Fog of the Seasons' End, Alex La Guma
Major Gentl and the Achimota Wars, Kojo Laing
The Grass is Singing, Doris Lessing
No Past No Present No Future, Yulisa Amadu Maddy
In the Hour of Signs, Jamal Mahjoub